A SHADOWS WRAITH

Twisted Tales

J B ARNOLD

For my Pops. A day doesn't pass without you in my thoughts.

AUTHOR'S NOTE

Thank you, reader, for your time and attention with A Shadow's Wraith. Without you, I wouldn't be able to produce these twisted tales. If you enjoyed this piece of fiction, please consider writing a brief review so others can learn about your experience (Amazon and/or Goodreads). A few kind words are the greatest gift you can send my way. Again, I write for you, not for the fame or the money. Thank you again for your continued support with my writing career. Until next time, stay creepy and twisted, peeps.

CONTENTS

It's right behind me
Hiding in the darkness
Its mocking laughter
Blaming me for its doing

It follows, chases me
A constant reminder
A tormenting memory
Of who I've become

Prologue

The Halloween Bash

A slight stagger appeared with each step as they strolled down the sidewalk—the euphoric effects of the pre-party on full display. Some booze layered with a hit from the glass pipe kick-started the cool fall evening. With their flawed attempts to escape reality, they continued forward on their way to the bash—the Halloween party they had looked forward to all year.

Claudia giggled into the brisk night, leaning into him—her beau and daughter's father. Her nose nuzzled under his stubbled chin, smelling his cologne. The one he only wore on special occasions, nights like this. She always felt safe in his strong, brawny arms, knowing he wouldn't let a fly hurt her. She knew he would save her from falling too. No matter how inebriated the two were, and both planned on making tonight an epic brain-cell-killing session, he had always saved her—a knight amongst the bumbling thieves they ran with.

As they walked, Frank held her close, arm draped around her lower back and gently gripping her side, cautious of the red pointed tail of her costume. He declined to wear a matching one, sporting the dual horns on his forehead instead. He held her with purpose, knowing how clumsy she was in heels. The *click-clack* echoed on the concrete with each stride, and his grin could be seen from the heavens as they neared the house. This wasn't a neighborhood they would walk through willingly any other night, but tonight was an exception.

Rounding a street corner, the pulsing beat of music pounded into the night, accompanied by peals of drunken laughter. Cars lined both sides of the street, and hordes of costumed partygoers were shuffling toward the house. Frank stopped at the chain-link fence guarding the property, directing his lazy stare at his queen, his love, which she returned. They shared the moment for several seconds, knowing they were on the verge of an epic evening. Then, still walking side by side, Frank ushered Claudia toward Martinez's front door.

Hector Martinez was a low-time heroin dealer from the Heights District, along with a string of other escapades. He was notorious for cutting his product and slinging it around the neighborhood at bargain basement prices—the only prices the addicts and homeless could gather in this section of the East Side. Secretly, Frank hated the guy, but when the cravings hit, beggars can't choose who they dine with. And the man's Halloween parties were legendary.

Opening the front door, Cypress Hill's "How I Could Just Kill a Man" struck them with force. Strobe lights pulsed and spun in the darkness, and billows of smoke lifted through the meandering lights. A few neighborhood girls, clad in makeshift angel and cop costumes, danced in the center of the front room while their dates huddled around in groups of threes and fours savoring beers.

As they entered, a large man, belly as round as a barrel, acknowledged Frank with minimal genuineness. He wore a black beanie that matched the rest of his wardrobe, pulled down tightly near his bloodshot eyes. One of Hector's boys, an important man in the circle.

He leaned into Frank, speaking over the thumping bass and chorus, "Better have brought some shit with you, Franky, and my money. This isn't a free buffet or a charity."

Frank returned the gesture, leaning in and elevating his voice. "Just here for a good time, Miguel. Here to celebrate with my queen." He glanced Claudia's way, delivering a grin before redirecting toward the behemoth. "I've got you, man."

Pulling back, he reached into the fifth pocket of his Levi's where he had hidden twenty dollars, nearly all the money he had to his name. As he waited for Claudia to finish with her makeup earlier in the night, he had folded the bill and stuffed it away, knowing Miguel would hit him up for the debt. It would at least give them some leeway, a short leash to sample some other delicacies.

Miguel held out a beefy tattooed palm, accepting the crumpled bill with a blank face. He had a reputation for neither theatrics nor patience. After stuffing the money into his pocket, he leaned in once more. "Be careful, Franky."

With the act complete and satisfaction teetering on the edge, the large man sauntered away, bobbing his head to the beat. He rejoined some associates sitting in lawn chairs staged along the room's far wall.

Frank turned to Claudia and pulled her close, cradling the love of his life in a tight embrace. He knew everything would be okay.

2

An hour later, Frank ambled through a dark hallway, leaning heavily against the drywall. He had bumped into a few acquaintances throughout the home, sampling the sweet miscellany they offered: a mild hit of acid, and he even choked down some pills with a warm beer like a seasoned vet. None of it was free, of course. No, if you wanted a taste of the goods, you had to give to get. He had peddled his quarter ounce of pot to the brink of emptiness, but he couldn't care less about the weed.

The hallucinogens were flowing now, steering him, carrying him forward toward the kitchen. His mind warped, folding with ecstasy. The colors and shapes. The release.

He had left Claudia earlier in the night, opting to roll solo in search of the elusive candy scattered around Martinez's place. He'd find her later; they always met back up during benders like this. But he wasn't alone. He was never alone anymore. A forsaken weight rode with him, unbeknownst to his psyche. Darkness. It cradled his nape and shoulders, lingering in his wake, pulling him downward into the depths of misery. An addict's sidekick.

As he inched closer, the kitchen lights illuminated a sliver of the hall. He stumbled forward into the room, but somehow, he brought the parasitic wave of darkness with him. The quilt of blackness clung to him like a cloak before releasing and scurrying up the walls to hide from the warmth. Wisps of gray sifted up through the air, vanishing into nothingness as if it had never been there.

Stepping forward, he inadvertently kicked an empty beer bottle, sending it scattering along the linoleum floor. It spun clockwise, spinning effortlessly, with no end in sight. Around and around. Frank's eyes watched it spiral, perplexed by the veils of hues shimmering from the object. Iridescence gleamed and shone with each turn.

Laughter rang out from his left. The sounds muffled and distorted, breaking his sloppy gaze. He slowly craned his neck toward the source, taking in the scene and all its splendor. Hector Martinez sat at a round table, flanked by others: soldiers and low-time corner dealers. Empty beers and a half-full tequila bottle littered the table's surface, nearly blanketing the treasure in the center. Nearly.

A plastic baggie sat on the table, tied off with a green twist tie. It teased Frank with its wicked smile. The sticky tar within winked at him like a high school crush. His old friend, yet his nemesis. His true love. The one thing he cared about more than Claudia. His cancer.

Even with the glowing bulbs overhead, the burden clinging to Frank returned at the sight. It whispered in his ear, tempting him with false promises while its flesh smoldered in the light. But it held firm, blanketing his neck and shoulders in sulfuric rot. It savored the view, knowing how close it was now.

As Frank stood there, eyes drawn to the bag's contents, its owner confronted the newcomer to the kitchen, breaking the lecherous moment. "The fuck you doin' here, Franky? See any other bitches in the room?"

Silence. Even the rhythmic pulse of the speakers drowned and drifted away.

Frank, stifled and frozen, searched for the words. Shock and fear pierced the synthetically-driven euphoria. He locked onto the man sitting at the table, seeing his stoic posture, counting the man's fingertips that gently touched one another. Contempt and loathing smothered the room's atmosphere. Hector never hid his true opinion about people.

Minutes seemed to pass, a timeless countdown with no end, before Hector released a snicker. It was deep and vengeful, like a hyena's laugh after the kill. "*Pinche ratón.*" The man slapped the table with a fierce palm as his counterparts joined in on the gag, shuffling about in their seats, pointing and jeering Frank's way.

The butt of a joke. That's all Frank was to them. A low-life burnout begging for scraps. He had no place at this table, but the cravings were too strong. He felt a rancid breath next to his ear, urging him to test the waters. The slithering tongues attached to the voices tempted him, promising bliss.

His eyes darted to the bag again, and this time, Hector knew Frank's intentions.

"Oh, look at this, fellas." Hector slowly raised out of his chair, glancing at the counterparts flanking his left and right. "This motherfucker wants a taste of the candy. A lick of the *chiva*."

Frank's twitchy eyes shot to Hector before landing once more on the bag. Every instinct told him to turn around and walk away, get out of there and find Claudia, but the taunts still rang in his ears. He could feel the push escorting him to the dinner table. Ignoring the dangers, he stepped forward, seeing the corners of Hector's mouth curl upward.

3

A short time later, Frank left the candy store, shouldering his passenger and carrying a new debt. The weight pulled him back down the hall, slipping past closed doors. From within these rooms, moans of elated pleasure shuddered, but he ignored them. He had what he needed, even with the price attached. Hector was a problem for another day. The toxins pumped freely, flowing through his bloodstream, and he loved it. This was the euphoria he coveted.

Another closed door stood at the end of the hall. Light penetrated the cracks of the doorframe, calling to Frank like a beacon. He shuffled forward, rounding an embraced couple, accidentally brushing against them. The man broke free from his partner's lips and uttered something in Spanish, a slur Frank was very familiar with. Thick white paint covered the man's face, along with some red streaks curling upward from the corners of his mouth. Another Joker amongst the host's royal family. Frank dismissed the man without a word, aiming for the calling door.

The doorknob felt warm in his grip as he twisted it, jarring it open a few inches. As he pushed it inward, the light from the room's ceiling flooded the hallway, forcing Frank to guard his eyes with a hand. But he pushed on, opening the door in a wide arc. Then he saw her.

The radiant glow from above revealed a scene dripping with pain. His eyes bulged at the sight, and his heart hammered in his chest. There, on the dingy floor of Hector's bathroom, was the only thing he loved as much as the junk sifting through his veins. Claudia. She lay on her side, facing the doorway, eyes frozen in a sea of fear. Tendrils of drying blood marched from her nostrils, pooling on the cold floor. She wasn't breathing.

Frank felt the icy grip of paralyzation forcing him to hold his sight. But through the bubbling anguish, something else broke him loose from the bonds. Plagues of darkness crept in from every direction. Slender black fingers tickled his flesh while those familiar, taunting whispers returned, urging him, guiding him to the nefarious truth.

Rushing inside, Frank knelt next to her on the ground, lips trembling at the sight. "Claudia. Claudia. Baby, wake up." He fixated on her eyes—glassy, lifeless orbs. They stared in his direction, casting a spell of guilt and misery.

He slid his arm under her limp head, pulling it toward him, then gently patted her cheek. "No, no, no, no. Baby, wake up. Wake up, Claudia."

His downcast stare hovered over his girl, his love, seeing the blood, the remnants of powder sullying her nostrils, the void of color in her skin. This was utter pain, and it was self-inflicted. Why had he left her?

Time stilled as he sat there on the floor, cradling her head in his lap. The rapturous high from moments before melted away with each longing sob. Those solemn cries slowly morphed into bellows of agony, earning an audience outside the bathroom. Partygoers from all walks of life clad in their demented skins and costumes followed the screams to the source, where they witnessed the truth: a dead junkie and the loser she came with. What they couldn't see was the infernal cancer clinging to every scream.

With his mind splintered and his heart in tatters, the shadows slunk forward, lapping up the excreted misery and feeding on his pain. Talons and teeth took grip, holding him in a tight, loving embrace. And they would never let go.

4

Martinez caught wind of the dead woman minutes later. He sprang to action, killing the stereo and ordering his henchmen to rid the home of the corpse, but it was too late. One of the many sultry nurses at the gig had already panicked and hysterically dialed 911. Her raging, drunken babbling prompted a rapid response from the sheriff's substation a few blocks away. Before anyone could mop up the mess, blue and red rotating lights painted the home's exterior while most of the indulged escaped through the back alley, scattering in the night like roaches.

Deputies wearing black vests emblazoned with the county's signature KCSD (Kern County Sheriff Department) stormed the house, firearms brandished and sporting detestation in their eyes. In no time, they swept through the home, forcing the few remaining lone individuals to lie on the floor, fingers interlocked behind their heads. Hector included.

With the risk cleared, two officers sidestepped down the hall, approaching the bathroom with caution. Both had their gun sights aimed at the man sitting on the floor. Frank hadn't even noticed the chaos unfold until shouts and orders filled his ears, swatting away the loathsome whispers. With tears streaking his cheeks, he glanced up toward the door's opening, seeing judgment and hate. This was real, and there was no high that could shake the pain.

After a brief scuffle, the officers slammed Frank onto the hallway carpet, hands pinned behind his back. As they cuffed him, his swollen eyes followed a set of EMTs bolting past and through the bathroom's doorway. Resuscitation began immediately, but he knew she was already gone. Her warmth and aura faded in his arms, leaving only the torments, laughter and mockery. In that moment, while he watched a series of pointless chest compressions, genuine pain announced its arrival.

Through the hysteria, a small, youthful voice shattered Frank's numbness. One that didn't fit the scene. "Mommy?"

At first it was soft, passive, but after that nervous voice neared, the innocence sifted away like ash in the wind, and chaos ensued.

As soon as the screams began, he knew it was her. He craned his neck, trying to roll onto his side, eyes darting down the other end of the hall. And then he saw her. His daughter, Chloe. Her blue eyes shot past him, locking onto the tragedy within the bathroom. The pain, fear, and suffering emitting from her throat tore him to shreds, and he was helpless to protect her from the scene.

"Chloe! What are you doin' here? Why aren't you at—"

"Get that fuckin' kid out of here!" The officer kneeling on his spine cut him off. Frank's gaze snapped upward, drawn to the deputy hovering over him. Spittle flew from the man's lips with each order. His frantic gestures aimed toward the shocked little girl in the purple hoodie.

Her stare shot to her father. "Daddy!"

Before another officer could grasp the six-year-old, she bolted forward, weaving through the calamity of bodies. But just as she nearly reached her detained father, an arm whipped around her tiny waist, halting her and pulling her backward. Her frail arms lunged for him, reaching for safety, for embrace, but her fingertips never made contact. Amid the commotion, her petite frame was whisked away, lost in a whirlwind of kicks and flails. And all Frank could do was watch and mirror her agonizing screams as the deputies lifted him to his feet and escorted him out of the house.

Time was nonexistent as Frank sat in the back of a sheriff's cruiser, voidness smothering the drugs in his system. He was numb, except for a throbbing pain in his abdomen, the result of a nightstick strike while resisting the officers. Another check mark on his arrest record for the evening. The authorities wast-

ed no time in listing his indictments: under the influence, possession with intent, and charges related to child endangerment
and wrongful death.

In a matter of minutes, the world stripped his life away, and
he felt so small, so alone, yet he wasn't. Still clinging to him
was his darkness, loitering and laughing at his expense the entire
time.

He stared out the window, watching the shit show come to
an end, not able to rationalize how bad he had fucked up.

PART ONE

THE SON

1

CHESS

He studied the board, eyes darting over the cheap, plastic pieces. With each wavering pass, uncertainty wept like an open wound. A subtle breath escaped through his teeth as he gripped the bishop with his thumb and index finger. He held the piece with grit, cogs spinning before finally committing. Years had passed since he'd last played, and his rustiness streaked through the tough demeanor his face attempted to portray. A facade of confidence.

His father sat in the chair across the table, hunched over, watching with amusement and a tinge of disappointment. Slowly, his frail hands came together just under his chin, fingertips touching. His gaze fell to the board as his son completed the move, knowing the match was almost over. With a weak grin, he lifted his stare, locking onto his son once more. The victory wouldn't be rewarding, though. So many afternoons and evenings in the past, he sat with his son playing this beloved game. The game his father taught him a generation ago. Teaching. Coaching. Criticizing.

Tension hung in the air as they locked eyes, poker faces on full display until the old man abruptly shattered it.

"When was the last time you played, Mikey?"

"It's Frank, Pops." He brushed the moment away, not allowing the confusion to latch on and string him up. "Mikey's been gone a long time. Years."

The old man stared at him, considering the news. "Yeah, yeah. I know." He paused, smacking his lips. "I know that. You haven't been playing much, have you, Franky?"

The son's face slacked, not surprised by the question oozing with indictment. Regardless of his efforts, his play was sloppy. He knew that, and now his father's advantage doubled, tripled possibly. The onslaught was in mid-swing, but maybe he could surprise himself. Maybe he could surprise the old man, take a piece or two and survive long enough to earn a humble nod.

"Been a while, Pops. A long time." Franky lifted his head, posture stiffening. "But I'm good. I've still got my bearings. If I go down, it'll be swinging. You taught me that, remember?" Based on the nurse's news upon his arrival and the confusion with names, he didn't know if his father remembered anything.

The old man's eyes narrowed, the deep wrinkles of his sun spotted forehead flattening out as he studied his son. "Sounds like something I'd say." He left it at that, returning his attention to the board before moving his bishop. "Check."

"Shit." The word mumbled from Frank's lips, fearing the charade had sprung a leak and the vessel was taking on water.

"Well, what are you going to do, boy?" Scratching his face, the old man stared through the small window on the closed door.

Frank's attention volleyed between the board and his father, loathing each sight: the shitty position his pieces were in and the smirk crossing the old man's lips.

How can he remember how to play? He doesn't even know my name.

Frank shook off the thoughts, knowing the death blow was one wrong move away. Instinctively, he reached for a pawn, advancing a square and blocking the bishop. A humble sacrifice in this ancient game of strategy and wit.

After a few moments of silence, he watched his father revisit the board without a hint of emotion.

"You know you just fucked up, right, Franky?"

The accusatorial words forced a furrowed brow, along with some speculation. "What the hell are you talking about? I'm great. Maybe you're about to fuck up? I've got you on the run, old man. On the ropes and heading down for the count." The words flowed from his lips like a meandering stream.

A raspy chuckle sprang from the old man's throat. "Boy, you really can't see it, can you? That's always been your problem, Mikey. You've always played so offensive, going for the kill and failing to see my traps. Thinking with your cock and not your brain."

The jab forced a dry laugh, and he ignored the name. No need to beat a dead horse. His father always had a way with words, even during his youth. Apparently, the colorful language had resonated because he could still recall the countless after-school detention sessions.

Confidence was boiling, filling his veins. "Maybe you didn't see my trap, Pops." Frank paused, erasing the softness of his features. "But you will. It's about to spring."

"Really?" The word came out more like "Bullshit."

Frank rolled his shoulders, trying to hold his father's stare without buckling. Even with the man's advanced age and diagnosis, he still carried some clout. "Yeah, really."

"Well then . . ." His father leaned forward, reaching for his queen without breaking eye contact. He gripped the piece with shaky fingers, making sure not to move it. "Game's over, Franky. Checkmate."

Frank followed the piece as it slid across the board, eyes widening with each passing second. The old man never bluffed, so deep down, the words spoke only the truth. With a tilted head, he eyed his king, tracing imaginary lines across the board, searching for the reaper's scythe. Even with the piece in place, he still couldn't take apart where he'd gone wrong.

"How?" he demanded. As the words exited his mouth, the bright fluorescent lighting above flickered, delivering the room into darkness on two occasions before stabilizing. Ignoring the anomaly, he latched onto his father. He expected to see smugness dripping from the man, but what he found forced his pulse to skip a beat.

"Pops?" He leaned in, remembering the episodes the nurse mentioned before he entered the hospital room.

With no response, he stood, leaning even closer over the chessboard. "Pops, can you hear me? You okay?"

He reached out, waving his hand in front of the old man's face. Still nothing. His father sat there, slack-jawed with a blank stare.

Frank pulled his hand away, concern piling on. "I'm . . . going to get the nurse, Pops," he whispered, turning to eye the small glass window in the room's door. Through the opening, he could see the nurses' station. Two women wearing blue scrubs stood there, exchanging a cell phone and mirroring each other's laughs.

As he broke through the moment and swiveled to leave, shock struck him like a viper's bite. The cold tendrils of his father's fingers clung to his wrist, squeezing it like a vise. With a fluttered heart, his view flicked back to his father, staring in disbelief at the old man. The catatonic episode dissolved, wiped away as if it had never occurred. His father sat there, clad in his indignant smirk, eyes gleaming.

After a few seconds, the old man tugged on his son's wrist, ushering him back to his abandoned seat. "Where are you going, Franky? Game's over. Checkmate."

Frank inched forward, slowly lowering himself into the wooden chair, unable to break his gaze.

Was that the dementia?

After delivering a comforting nod, his father's constricting grip finally released.

"Pops, you all right?" Frank's voice wavered like static. "Do you know what just happened?"

"You never saw it coming, did you, boy?" The old man smiled, exposing a mouth of yellow teeth.

"Pops, listen. Did you fall asleep or something? The nurse told me about these episodes you've been experiencing . . ." Frank's voice trailed off as he struggled to find the right words.

In an unexpected turn, the old man doubled over, coughing phlegmatically. Frank bolted from his seat to aid, applying gentle strikes between the old man's bony shoulder blades. "Pops, Pops. You okay?"

The spell ended within seconds, and Frank's father cast his eyes toward his son, bloody spittle dribbling from his mouth. "I'm fine, dammit. I'm fine." He used the back of his hand to wipe away the mess. "I'm fine."

Frank dropped his eyes, staring at the linoleum floor, shaking his head. "I'm sorry. I didn't know it was this bad. I should have come sooner."

The "I'm fine, dammit. I'm fine" chant echoed through the room before silence snuffed it out. While Franky stared at the floor, allowing guilt to rush over him, the old man's stare shifted to the door's window. He wondered what day it was and why he was in this room.

2

Four days ago, a team of EMTs rolled the old man through the emergency room doors after responding to a frantic 911 call. A neighbor found him unconscious in the front yard, wearing his classic blue plaid robe and matching slippers. An uncharacteristic fall after retrieving the morning paper. An act he had performed thousands of times.

The responders found no form of identification on the unconscious man, relying merely on his home address to track down a family member. Once admitted, and after hours of searching for a working phone number, the hospital finally located Frank Collins, Jr., the old man's only living son.

A little after two p.m. that day, Frank drove through an impoverished neighborhood of East Bakersfield searching for a delinquent, blue Ford Mustang. The vehicle had not been at the registered owner's apartment building, so he ventured out into the jungle. Repossessing vehicles was dangerous work, but it provided a steady income, as modest as it was. And after the felonies, he was lucky to find a job, let alone keep his driver's license.

While prowling the streets, the phone sitting in the cab's center console sprang to life in a violent hum. The eruption of sound sent a tremor through Frank's body, and he nearly steered the tow truck into a fire hydrant. After collecting himself and pulling the truck over, he answered the call.

A PR director from Bakersfield Memorial Hospital was on the other end. Frank sat there, listening to the woman's macabre words, her judgmental tone as she explained the old man's symptoms. She even made a declaration of urgency for action, each word painted with imperativeness. Either the old man would die in his hospital room or the comfort of a loved one's home. With indifference, he agreed to come down as soon as possible.

After the call ended, a myriad of emotions flooded Frank's mind. The suffocating feelings started with worry, accompanied by fear. But after leveling his breathing, a little strategy his PO suggested he learn, pique crept inside, washing away the empathy. A deep sigh sounded in the truck, and Frank rubbed his stubbled chin.

After his arrest two years prior, estrangement ensued between him and his father, both convinced it was the better path. Only a handful of words had passed in the last six months since his release. And he was fine with it.

His life was different now, and he finally felt like the ship had righted itself. He was employed, clean, and, for the first time, motivated for more than just the next hit. And so close to getting custody of his daughter. He didn't need to be dragged back down into the gutter, dealing with family shit. Family he didn't recognize anymore. His old life, the sins, the memories needed to remain buried. Reincarnation was necessary, a rebirth, to say. Yet here he was, knowing where this ride would lead him. And unfortunately, there was no one else climbing aboard.

The guilt eventually vanquished his will after three days, forcing him to face the demons of his past. It was his day off, and he couldn't hide any longer. That morning, after slamming a Red Bull in his El Camino, he strolled through the metal detectors of the hospital's entrance, flashed his ID, and signed the visitor form. He even sported the little sticker the security officer gave him on his chest, documenting his name and what room awaited his arrival. He hated every second.

And now, as he sat there in the depressing hospital room, absorbing the strikes of guilt and pain, suppressing the ill feelings of abandonment, he pondered how he could have allowed selfishness to take control. This was his father, his kin. He thought their relationship was dead, but some things never die.

Frank broke loose from the self-loathing and despair, leaving the firmness of the seat and paced the room. He rubbed his eyes with his palms, searching for answers to unknown questions. But deep down, he already knew what lay ahead. His father was sick, and luckily for him, the burden now rested in his hands.

He paused his pacing and diverted his stare back at the old man, pity and regret fueling his words. "I'm sorry. I'm sorry for all this shit. For not being here, for not coming right away." His words choked up as he watched the old man tilt his head and smack his lips. Tears welled in his eyes at the sight.

Frank stepped forward, his chin dipping further with each step. "I'm going to get you out of here. Take you home. Take care of you. Okay?" He figured his words fell on deaf ears, but maybe this could right the past, abolish the pain, the memories. Maybe.

Laughter rang out behind him, slicing through the room. Frank jerked his head around toward the door now ajar, blinking back welled eyes. A dark-haired, heavyset nurse poked her head through the opening. Her forced smile waned as she locked onto Frank, but something else lingered there, just below the surface.

"It's time for Mr. Collins's medicine, sir. Do you mind if I see him in private for a few moments?" The words came out more like a declaration than a query.

"Umm . . . umm, yeah. Yeah, sure. That's fine." Frank smoothed out his shirt's wrinkles with his palms, watching the woman enter the room. As she brushed past him, he turned, latching onto his father, wondering if this would be his life now: feeding his father pills every few hours, swapping out the diaper the poor man wore, sitting for hours on end, getting murdered at chess.

As the nurse started in with some small talk, easing the old man's nerves, Frank backpedaled toward the door. "I'll be outside, Pops. Right outside, okay?" Either the old man didn't hear him or he was too preoccupied with the nurse. There was no rebuttal, no acknowledgment.

Frank slipped out the door without another thought. A little stroll down the corridor might level his mind, get some blood flowing. Maybe he could clear his head, think about what he was considering: taking on this demanding task, this potential burden. But what about his daughter, his job? The constant harassment from his PO? How could he balance any of it? These ill thoughts looped in his mind as he sauntered through the halls, completing a full circle right back inside his father's room.

He stood there in the hall, staring through the door's window. Hesitation held him firm in place. He had no answers for his thoughts, for the future. All he knew was that everything was about to change.

A long breath blew from his lips, shedding the constricting nerves. He stepped forward, fingers reaching for the door handle. Before he could grasp it, the door sprang open, forcing him to stride to the left.

The dark-haired nurse stood on the door's other side, leaving his father's room. She came to a halt, cheap sneakers squeaking against the freshly polished linoleum. She was a little startled at Frank's proximity.

"Sorry, miss. Excuse me." Frank smiled, expecting one in return while he held the door open. She overcame the surprise, glued to Frank. She held the odd glare for a moment, excavating Frank's rough demeanor before her lips curled. It lacked authenticity.

With that, she stepped through the doorframe, bound for the nurses' station. Her eyes left the old man's son, dismissing him without a sound.

Frank ignored the impertinent look. During those dark years of drug dependency, desensitization became a growing weed, blocking out care. But he needed answers, something to lean on. He could give a rat's ass what she thought about him. As she strolled away, he followed, catching her and matching her swift strides before cutting off her path. "Miss. Miss, can I ask you something?" He held up his hands, palms open. "Some questions about my father?"

She stopped, annoyance masking her rigid stance. "Sir, I've got other patients to see. If you need some answers, ask one of them." She lifted her chin, gesturing at the two nurses sharing the cell phone. "They can help you, okay?"

The smug tone forced a response. "What the hell is this shit?" Frank squared his jaw, allowing his temper to boil. "I just need to know what's wrong with my father. I'm sure you've been assisting him all week, right? I'm family, and I need answers."

The nurse looked around the hall, cautious of loitering ears. "Family?" She scoffed, letting the tone match her glare. "Is that what you call yourself?" She crossed her arms, eyes narrowing. "That poor man has been in that room for four days, alone. Management contacted you on Tuesday. It's Friday, if you didn't know. Family?" She snickered.

The words stung, but she was right. The overpowering guilt justified that. "Miss, I just need some help. Please. I need to know what to expect."

The nurse swayed a little, listening to Frank's plea, watching his ego spill onto the floor. "Sir, I have to go. Actual *families* need my help."

Again, Frank held up those calloused hands, blocking her from rounding him. "I . . . I don't know what the hell I'm doing." He paused, leaning to the right, looking over her shoulder at his father's room. "Please, help me understand."

She could hear the concern hovering in his voice. The disturbed texture of his words. She had already judged this book's cover, but empathy be damned. After a subtle shake of her head, she responded, "Honestly, his dementia is deeply rooted. Every patient is different, but we don't know what these episodes are. We haven't seen them before. The neurologists are running tests, but nothing has come back yet. Epilepsy possibly?"

"You guys don't know?" The words came out painted in layers of qualm. "Isn't this a hospital? Why don't you know what's happening to my father?"

"Sir, this disease is unpredictable. No two patients are the same, but we're helping him, comforting him."

"How are you comforting him when you don't know what's happening?" He held out his hands, expecting a response.

Her stance stiffened once more. "What is your name?"

"Frank. I'm Frank, just like him. Frank Junior."

That indignant stare returned. "Well, thank you for coming to visit, Frank Junior. When we know something, we'll be in contact. Try to stick around. He needs you. Your father needs you, 'kay."

With that, she brushed past him, leaving him standing alone in the hall. Time seemed to still, slowing to a rhythmic pulse that matched the sound of her soles striking the shiny floor, getting fainter and fainter with each passing heartbeat. His stare followed her, watching as she strolled away. Above him, the canned lighting flickered, bringing him back.

His head shifted upward, taking in the dancing bulbs, the cross paneling of the ceiling. "What the hell's wrong with this place?" he mumbled before crossing the space and reaching for the door handle of his father's room.

3

Quietly entering the room, Frank found his father in slumber. The old man lay in his bed, head drooping to the side, mouth parted; a faint snore flowed from the cavity. The nurse must have tucked him in after delivering his medicine. Frank made his way to the table, watching the old man's brittle chest rise and fall. As he took his seat, his mind blistered with scenarios and what-ifs.

What the hell was he thinking? How could he drop everything and care for this man? This stubborn, self-righteous SOB who never showed him an ounce of love growing up. This man who criticized and chipped away at every accomplishment, every win. The same man who turned his back when the addiction became too much to control. The arrest. How?

He stared at his father, allowing the feelings to simmer. Memories of childhood flooded his mind, remembering the harsh words, the belts, and fists. Moments passed while he lounged in his pool of pity, hating every tormenting swing of the pendulum. This wasn't fair, but there wasn't another soul who could take this on. The bloodline was tapped.

The hospital room seemed to close in on him, walls gliding forward, and with it, the lights continued their eccentric behavior. His stare darted to the ceiling, watching as the illumination faded, delivering darkness in its wake. But unlike the previous occurrences, the void remained. As he rose from the chair, he thought he heard something. It wasn't his father's snoring or the machinery in the room. No, he knew those sounds. This sounded more like a whisper, faint and distorted.

In an instant, a brilliant flash of light filled the room, illuminating every corner in a radiant white glow. The soft hum of electricity echoed in the air. The room was imbued with a soothing scent of tranquility, as Frank's father lay there, peacefully asleep, his breaths rhythmic and calm.

2

EL CAMINO

TWO HOURS LATER, FRANK steered his El Camino into the passenger loading zone just outside the hospital's glass doors, neatly hugging the line of white paint. He chalked up the anomaly in his father's room to stress, suppressing it away without another thought. He was good at that, and he had other things to worry about. With the discharge papers signed and the case manager's meeting in the rearview, his new life was in full swing. He had some planning to do, not to mention the continual reference to hospice care by every staff member he interacted with.

He stood there outside the hospital, leaning over the car's roof, waiting for his father to be wheeled through those doors. Waiting and worrying. Unconsciously, his fingers rapped the roof's oxidized steel, anticipation festering.

After a few minutes, movement from beyond the glass caught his sight. A tall, massive man dressed in black scrubs pushed a wheelchair toward the exit. The doors parted in unison and the view struck like an uppercut. Frank's father sat there, hunched over as the massive nurse wheeled him forward.

Frank silently conveyed his gratitude to the man by nodding, expressing his thanks without a word.

Once the wheels came to a stop, the nurse's eyes hovered over the car, taking in the rust, the missing fender. "Mister Frank Collins, I assume." He smiled as his eyes drifted up, staring at Frank.

"Yeah, that's me," Frank stated, almost unconvinced.

The man hesitated before continuing. "The case manager filled me in on your father's condition. I know this can't be easy, seeing a loved one like this, but my humble heart blooms knowing you are here. He will be safe, cherished." The man's smile widened, revealing a missing tooth in his lower jaw.

"I'm gonna do my best. Honestly, I don't know what I'm doing or how to care for him, but —" Frank dropped his head. Flashes of the past strobed in his mind. The dark years. The years of heroin and blood.

"You will do fine, Mister Collins." The powerful statement brought him rushing back to the moment. "It is your will, I know it."

Frank shook off the rancid memories and let the words sink in before delivering another nod. He wasn't sure he could handle this, but there was no cooling-off period here. And something about the man's assurance sifted through the self-doubt plaguing his thoughts. Slowly, he rounded the vehicle's bed, strolling toward the large man and his waiting father.

"But—" He paused, rethinking his words. "But what if I can't do this? What if it's too big for me, too daunting?" His stare darted toward his ailing father, noticing the old man had dozed off. "I mean, I can barely take care of my sorry ass."

The nurse reached out and clasped Frank's shoulder. "You will have success because you must. He is your kin, your blood. It will be trying, but you will fill this man with light. Fulfill his final days."

The tone and delivery sent radiating waves throughout the space, lifting the suffocating veil of doubt. Frank stared at the man, feeling the confidence percolate. Maybe he *could* do this. Those dark years of needles, begging, and stealing were over, buried six feet under. He was a new man, molded by prison and sobriety. A changed man, regardless of the scars still piercing his heart.

"Thank you." Frank's eyes gleamed, allowing the aura to surround him. "What was your name?"

The nurse released his grasp, standing a little taller. The glint in his eye danced. "My mother named me Kwame many years ago." He brought his hands together, fingertips and palms touching, and bowed his head.

"Kwame. Thank you, Kwame," Frank whispered.

The nurse's head lifted, faith and conviction spiraling within his light brown eyes. "The Lord's light will guide you through the darkness."

Frank couldn't respond, but he couldn't break the link either. He was a passenger on this ride. He stood there, a gentle sway in his stance, like a leafless branch on an autumn day.

The nurse known as Kwame slowly lowered his hands, and the devotional moment seemed to dissipate.

Frank shook off the feeling, looking around the parking lot. The afternoon sun forced a squint. "Thanks again, Kw-Kwame. Can you"—he paused, gesturing at his father and the wheelchair—"help me get him in the car?" Frank reached down and lifted the handle, swinging the door in a wide arc.

That contagious glint returned to the nurse's eyes, followed by a wide smile. "Indeed. Let the voyage commence." With that, Kwame bent over and swooped up Frank's father from the chair, cautious and gentle with each movement. He held the aged man, a beefy arm supporting his rail-thin legs while the old man's torso rested against the nurse's massive chest. With deliverance and care, Kwame lowered Frank's father into the car. He knelt, leaning into the cab, then secured the man's seat belt.

As he did, Frank noticed the nurse lean into his father's ear and whisper something. Something he couldn't make out, but his father seemed comforted by it. He tapped the nurse's bulky shoulder. A sign of good faith and trust.

Kwame stood and gently closed the car door, turning to take in Frank once more. "You will do fine. Remember, it is your will." He brought his hands together, mirroring the action from moments ago.

Without another word, Kwame gripped each push handle and rolled the wheelchair back toward the glass doors.

Once he was a few paces away, Frank called out to him, "Kwame. Kwame."

The nurse slowed to a stop, glanced back over his shoulder.

"What did you say to my father? You whispered something in his ear."

Kwame pivoted, turning sideways. "Ah, it was an old prayer for an old man. Something from my home country. A blessing."

"Can I . . . Can I hear it?" The words were soft, hopeful.

The nurse stood a little taller, lips curling again. "Of course." He stepped forward, closing the distance between the two before bowing his head. "*Nuru itashinda giza mchungaji wangu.*" As he completed the verse, he dipped his chin.

Frank allowed the foreign phrase to linger in his mind. He had never heard something so odd, yet so powerful. "What does it mean?"

"You will learn soon enough. The light will reveal the truth. Take care, Mister Collins." He nodded to Frank and took leave, rolling the wheelchair back through the doors.

Frank watched him until the man's figure disappeared from within.

2

The old man came around minutes later, jostled after the car struck a pothole. He stared around the cab, vision hazed and layered with segments of confusion. Incoherent mumbles flung from his thin, dry lips before he found his son. "Mikey? Mikey? What is this shit?"

Frank glanced over, considering the old man's worry and fidgeting fingers. Empathy rose in his core, but this shell was still his father, Frank Collins, Sr. "Nah, pops. It's Frank. Mikey's gone, remember?" He didn't mind repeating himself, knowing this would probably become a daily discussion.

The old man stilled and seemed to wither in place at the news. His view turned away from Frank, taking in the destitute nature of the neighborhood they drove through. He was silent, bottom lip quivering.

Seeing the old man's muddled gestures, Frank eased the vehicle to the right, throwing it in park next to the curb. He released his grip on the steering wheel and stared at the cab's roof for a few heartbeats, counting with each rhythmic thump. Another trick his PO employed that he now used to deflate the lingering anger and agitation.

After a sigh left his body, he addressed his father. "Hey, Pops. I'm taking you home, okay? It's going to be alright."

The old man broke his gaze from the window as he listened to the words. "Home? You're taking me back to my shitty shack?"

At least he remembers something, Frank thought.

"No, not your shitty shack, Pops. My shitty little apartment. You're going to stay with me for a while. I'm going to take care of you."

The old man allowed the words to simmer, averting his gaze to the windshield. After a few moments of silence, his rebuttal ensued as he assessed his son. "Why are we going to your place? What's wrong with my place? My place is fine."

"You're coming home with me because it's safer."

"But where's my stuff? My clothes, my records?"

"We'll get those things soon, Pops. All your stuff. I'll bring it later. But right now, we need to get home, get you situated."

Fuck, old man. Trying to help you here.

"I want to go home."

"I know, I know. I'm taking you to your new home. My home."

"I don't want to go to your shitty house. Take me to my place."

Frank puffed out his cheeks, knowing this conversation was going nowhere. "Pops, listen. I know you don't understand any of this, but it's for your own good. I'm here and I'm helping you." He could feel the annoyance bubbling.

Frank's father dropped his glare, a thin line penciled across his mouth. His view aimed out the passenger side window again, defiance leaking from his hunched posture.

Frank shook his head, pondering how much of this he could really take. They weren't even home and doubt had already crept back in, tearing at his insides.

"Where's Mikey?" the old man whispered after a minute.

"Pops!" The name exploded within the cab. "Mikey's not here. He's dead. He's been dead for years, all right." The volume and hostility in his son's voice forced the old man to cower, pressing against the car door, alert of danger.

Frank sat there, witnessing how his harsh words stripped away the old man's defenses, and the sudden outburst filled him with shame and guilt. Dropping his head, he rubbed his eyes with his palms, trying to soothe the ill emotions spreading through his body. Silent tension suffused the cab while Frank found his bearings. This wasn't the start he aimed for.

His view drifted back to his father, observing the nervous nature still lingering on the old man's face. It made him sick. "I'm sorry. That was wrong. That's not right, and it won't happen again, okay?" He meant every word, but he also knew how easy it was to fly off the deep end.

The old man remained silent, yet the rigidness of his brace slowly melted away. He took in the outside world, watching a woman walk past the car pushing a baby stroller. A grin crossed his lips as he inched forward, trying to get a glance at the tiny occupant.

Frank watched the transformation—the tension's gradual release—and it helped. The self-loathing plaguing his mind slipped away, and a mirrorlike grin formed as he observed his father. Everything would be okay. He could feel it.

Seconds later, he shifted into drive, steering the car down the empty street. They would be home in a few minutes, and the actual trials would begin. He was ready.

3

After unlocking the front door, Frank looked around his dark, barren apartment, breathing in the musty smell. He walked over to the curtains, pulling them open in a single swipe. Sunlight poured into the front room, vanquishing the dim and desolate as dust lingered in the air. He glanced around, a feeling of dejection swirling somewhere deep in his gut. He didn't have shit besides a recliner, an end table, and a pathetic excuse for a television in the front room. In the bedroom, there was little comfort to be found. His sagging comforter lay haphazardly in the corner, and a flickering lamp provided a meek and gloomy ambiance. This wouldn't do. He needed some help.

In addition to some resources, the case manager had warned him of the dangers within a home, including the culprits of most trips and falls: throw rugs, shoes, and pets. None were an issue here besides his cat, but the gray tabby, Max, only came home to eat. He also knew his father wouldn't be walking around much in his condition, if he could walk at all.

As he stood there, allowing feelings of self-pity and contempt to rise, the encounter with Kwame, the large nurse from the hospital, reentered his thoughts. The man's words, his assuredness, his illuminating aura snuffed out the cancerous thoughts looping within his mind. If he was going to do this, deliver his father to the light, he first had to believe in himself.

Leaving the front door ajar, he stepped out into the warm sunlight. Across the way, his eyes caught his neighbor, Damaris, or more affectionately, Mari. She stood in her doorway, staring in his direction, but stayed mute. They were close, and he could sense her investment in what was happening. It would have to wait, though. A nod and gentle wave would have to suffice for now.

Walking back to the car and his father, he reached into his back pocket, finding a business card. He lifted it to his face, reading the blazoned blue text: *Bakersfield's Hospice Care.* The case manager had already made arrangements with the local company, and their arrival time was within the hour. An electric hospital bed, bedpan, and daily nurse visits if needed. Free of charge because of the old man's condition and the tow company's meager insurance. Good old Medicare.

He tucked the card away and opened the passenger side door, cautious of scraping it against the curb. He knelt and peered inside. The old man sat there, his furrowed brow and constant shifting giving away his evident anxiousness.

"It's going to be okay, Pops. We're here. We're home."

4

"Set it up in the bedroom. Right in here, guys." Frank stepped forward through the bedroom doorframe, gesturing for the visitors to follow. "In the corner over there will be great. Right across from the other mattress."

Two employees from the hospice company followed him, one pushing the rolling bed and the other guiding it into the dainty, dimly lit room.

Frank watched the two for a moment as they positioned the bed and plugged into the outlet. A series of tests followed, assuring the bed was functional, so Frank removed himself from the scene. They'd show him the controls soon enough.

He stood in the hall just outside the bedroom, staring into the living room, staring at his father. Shortly after their arrival, he carried the old man inside and carefully positioned him in the recliner. The old man matched the look, locked onto his son. Confusion smothered the man's expression, accompanied by some discomfort as he fidgeted in the chair.

"What's wrong?" Frank asked, strolling forward. His strides ended when he reached the recliner, kneeling down to eye level. "Everything's okay. These guys are here to help."

The old man remained silent, eyes volleying between his son and the hallway. Frank could see the tremors pulsing through his weak limbs. "Hey? You okay, Pops?"

The old man lifted his arm, extending a bony index finger toward the hall behind them. "Piss." The word came out in a slur. "I've gotta piss."

"You have to piss?" Frank looked over his shoulder toward the hall. The bathroom was there on his left and the bedroom straight ahead. He hadn't really thought about how this would work. Everything had been trial and error at this point. "All right. Let's uh . . . let's get you in there."

For the second time in less than thirty minutes, Frank lifted his father from a seat, carrying the man. The old man only weighed a little over a hundred pounds in his withered condition, so the task was manageable, but Frank wondered how often he could do this. Bedpan, adult diapers? He'd find out soon enough.

With his father firmly square on the toilet, Frank exited the bathroom, giving his father a little privacy. He left the door jarred as he leaned against the hall's wall, waiting for the old man to finish. As he listened, his ears also made out the muffled sounds of the two men shuffling about in the bedroom, putting the final touches on their setup.

He leaned his head back against the drywall, mind teetering toward the future. How long did his father have left? Could a nurse come in and watch the old man while he worked? But mostly, he thought about his daughter, Chloe. How was this going to affect his efforts, his rights to custody?

The days leading up to his arrest still lingered in a haze. He couldn't remember shit, total blackouts. The booze, the powder, the needles. A suffocating bender without limits or remorse. That night, though, when paramedics arrived, followed by police, would always remain etched in his memory.

It was a Friday night, nearly two and a half years ago, when the shit hit the fan. Frank staggered through a dimly lit hallway, stepping over unconscious burnouts and addicts. He didn't know where he was, but the venom pulsing through his veins lifted his euphoria to levels he couldn't imagine. The colors, the shapes swirling. The beauty of life. The release. Endorphins and adrenaline matched each racing heartbeat, steering him to find more. But what he found that night was death and misery.

Whenever his eyelids closed, the scene came to fruition like a projector powering on, painting his mind in a layer of rot. As he opened a door that night, he found Chloe's mother, Claudia, lying on the bathroom floor, head turned and facing his direction. A stream of blood meandered from her nose, pooling on the cold ground. The sight was traumatizing, but her eyes shook his core. Those dead, bloodshot eyes stared straight through his soul. The crippling fear and panic of those eyes dropped him to his knees.

Reality slowly broke through the facade of chemically driven bliss, filling his heart with grief and despair. He sat on the floor with her in a timeless cycle, stroking her matted hair while the sobs echoed through the bathroom. With each ear-piercing wail, strobes of darkness pushed forward, surrounding him and his deceased girlfriend, cornering him, invading him.

And with the dark came the whispers. Faint, transparent whispers dangling in the blackness, coated in pain. Each was organic and distinguishable, plummeting him further into agony until the tormenting calls suddenly stopped.

Vibrant, artificial light flooded the room as the door sprang open. Frank shielded his eyes with a trembling hand as a pair of deputies rushed in, forcing him away from her. They slammed him on the floor just outside the bathroom, pinning him like a championship wrestler. He lay there, watching a group of paramedics hurdle over him and enter the bathroom. Straining his neck, he twisted his body in an attempt to catch a glimpse of them performing CPR, attempting to revitalize his girl, his love. The one who never judged, never labeled him for who he was. The mother of his child. That same child who was at the party. The six-year-old who was subjected to all the shit.

He could still hear Chloe's screams as she kicked and flailed, reaching for him. And the vision of the child's tears, her anguish and terror as the authorities pried her from his bloody grip, haunted his thoughts. No child should have to experience that.

That was Frank's rock bottom, his nadir. The authorities charged and booked him with drug possession, and he lost his world that night. His girl, his daughter, snuffed out, taken from him in an instant.

But that was the past. He served his time, fought for his path to renewal. He found a job and hadn't used since that night, even though the demons still lobbied. Redemption was on the horizon, and he could finally forgive himself if he had his little girl back. Chloe.

The rush of swirling water brought him back from his thoughts. From within the bathroom, his father mumbled incoherently. The sound made him chuckle with amusement.

Must be finished.

Moments later, he carried his father into the lone bedroom. The two hospice workers bound toward him, offering assistance, which he declined. This was his father, his family, his blood. Commitment and pride ushered him now, and the taste of absolution was distinct. He was ready to see this through.

5

With his father firmly entrenched in the comforts of the new bed, one worker, rail-thin with a sparse mustache, walked Frank through the controls. He even casually spoke to Frank's father and gently guided the old man's shaky fingers over each button, showing him how to use it. He demonstrated several positions with compassion and care, mindful of changes to the old man's demeanor. A natural in the industry.

They entered the living room together, intent on wrapping things up. After signing some papers and assuring the company's phone number was on hand, the two workers exchanged handshakes with Frank before exiting the apartment. The three stood outside for a few minutes, exchanging casual words, before the two workers ambled back into the white van and drove away.

As Frank closed the front door, staring at the light blue paint chipping away near the handle, isolation collapsed all around him like an avalanche. This was it, and he was alone for the journey.

Like clockwork, he secured each dead bolt before strolling back to the bedroom. He paused at the doorway, hands gripping the frame's corners. His eyes hovered in the dimly lit room, seeing how his father had kicked off most of his bedding and was attempting to rise.

Oh shit.

Frank rushed to the bedside, detangling the man's foot from a cluster of cotton and easing his tension. "What the fuck are you doing? You're going to hurt yourself." He started readjusting his father and the linens and blankets.

Incoherence flowed from the old man, rambles and nonsense flinging. "What is this shit?" He kicked his feet, trying to rise once more, but Frank gently guided him back into the bed. The old man stared around the dark room, confusion building up. "Where am I? Where'd you bring me? Take me home."

"Pops. Pops." Frank's voice rose, but he held back any frustration. It wouldn't do any good. He had to help the old man remember, massage the man's mind with reason and kindness. "You're with me. Franky. You're at my place."

Frank's father stopped his frantic actions, locking onto his son. His face went grim, yet after a few heartbeats and studying his son's face, he lay back down.

"Everything's okay." He let the words sink in, delivering subtle nods to ease the fit.

The old man didn't respond. He lay there, propped up by soft cushioned pillows, gazing his son's way, yet wrapped in disorientation.

Frank leaned in, returning his father's look. "Where the hell did you think you were going, anyway? You're already home." Frank noticed the old man's eyes glass over, and the built-up tension loitering in his manners slipped away. "Pops?"

Oh, no. Is this another one of those episodes?

The light fixture above their heads flickered for a moment before returning the room to its faint shine. Frank glanced up, wondering how long it had been since he last changed the bulbs. He reached for the fixture, slowly unscrewing a nut holding the plastic shield. As Frank was in the middle of the act, an unexpected sound echoed from below—something awful.

His eyes followed the shrill hiss, landing on his father. That glassy look painting the old man's face was nowhere to be found. In its place was something unexplainable. His father's eyes had rolled back in their deep, sunken sockets, revealing yellowing orbs of hate. The look, topped off with a morbid grin, forced Frank's heart to skip. The sight shook his core, and he staggered backward, unable to breathe. He fell to the floor, landing hard on his ass, pushing himself away from the bed.

From every direction, subtle whispers rang out, teasing his ears. Frantic, he searched for the sources, seeing nothing before landing back on the hospital bed.

Frank's father craned his neck, finding his son on the floor. Slowly, the old man pursed his lips, and that vengeful hiss leaked between his clenched teeth once more.

3

EMMA

MINUTES LATER, FRANK PACED the living room, cell phone clutched to his ear. He glanced into the bedroom with each erratic pass, checking on his father. The old man lay in his bed fast asleep. The episode ended seconds after it began, but it rattled him, and he immediately called the hospice company.

"No, no, no. Listen. This wasn't a seizure." Frank paused his frantic rant, listening to the nurse's voice pulse through the speaker. The woman's rebuttal did little to soothe his racing heart. "I don't know what the hell it was, lady, but I need someone to come over here." He rolled his eyes, hearing all the medical jargon and possibilities.

The two exchanged words for several minutes before the call finally ended. Before dropping his phone in his back pocket, he read the time: 1:47. A nurse would be at the apartment in an hour. A long hour filled with uncertainty and dread.

After repositioning the recliner, Frank sat in the living room, brooding. He leaned forward, staring into the darkness and unknown of the bedroom. The image of his father's horrid face looped in his mind, and he couldn't flush it out. It loitered there, stripping away his other worries. He couldn't shake it and time seemed to still.

A firm knock at the front door brought him about, followed by a warm, soft voice. Startled, he glanced around the room before craning his neck at the sound.

Is she already here? I just hung up the phone like ten minutes ago.

Pushing himself up from the chair, his eyes hovered over the armrest, seeing a tear. Unbeknownst to him, while waiting, his fingers had picked at a tuft, slowly shredding the stained fabric.

"Ah, shit. What the hell is this? How did I—" His mumbles paused, and he reached for his phone. As he brought it to his face, the screen bloomed to life. The time read 3:06.

How is it already three?

The voice from beyond the door called out again, and he swiveled, taking in the source's direction.

"Mister Collins. Are you in there?" A second series of knocks accompanied the inquiry. "Mister Collins?"

Frank scratched the side of his face while he sauntered forward, wondering where the last hour had gone. He disengaged each lock before gripping the knob and opening the door.

The owner of that calming voice stood on the other side, clad in yellow scrubs and a contagious smile. She nearly met Frank's height. "Mister Collins. Hi there. My name is Emma from Hospice Care." She extended her hand in a friendly gesture.

Frank stood there taking in the woman's features: subtle dimples and the soft crow's feet hiding behind her square, black glasses. She wore her auburn hair in a tight braid that hung down the middle of her back. Beauty wasn't the right term for her looks, but a charm existed there.

Frank mirrored Emma's action, reaching out and shaking her hand. His eyes drifted to the thin streak of gray weaved within her braid. "Yeah, hi there. I'm . . . I'm just Frank. No need for formalities."

Emma's light brown eyes softened at his words, and she delivered a nod. "Frank, it is, then. It's nice to meet you." She released his hand, returning the smile to her face. "I hear you need some *help* with your father."

The word stung a little. Ever since his release, he had scraped and clawed his way to this point without help. Independence, to say. Frank didn't want to seem anxious, but that word—help—brewed in the pit of his stomach, slowly churning. He also didn't want her to think he couldn't handle this, but the caseworker provided this resource. It felt too soon, though.

Frank rubbed the back of his shaved head, feeling defeat settle in, but cordiality was imperative here. "I'm glad you made it. I can't really explain what happened, but—"

Cutting him off, Emma chimed in with that melodic, soft voice, "Hey, no need for that now. That's why I'm here. I truly understand the commitment and difficulties this situation brings. You're not in this alone, Frank. I'm here for your father." She paused, eyes glimmering with confidence before continuing. "And you. Let's work together. I know how hard this journey is."

As the final piece of comfort left her lips, Frank felt the noose loosen. He was in over his head. He knew that the minute he brought his father home, but he wasn't in this alone. Hospice was here, or more importantly, Emma was here.

Frank dropped his head, staring at his scuffed Vans. He could feel the tension escaping with each breath. Looking up once more, he responded, trying to mimic her gentle stare, "Thank you. Really, this means a lot, miss."

Emma cocked her head slightly, taking in Frank, seeing the relief manifest before her. "Please, Frank, call me Emma. I have a feeling we'll be seeing each other often in the next few weeks."

Frank silently nodded, causing the conversation to fall into silence, yet his eyes spoke volumes and conveyed everything that Emma needed to understand.

"Well, then, Frank, I'm excited to meet your father."

2

Emma turned the knob and held it, pulling the door closed as she exited the bedroom. She slowly released it, praying the bolt wouldn't send a shattering click echoing through the space and awaken Frank's father. Additionally, she was hoping to find a few moments of privacy to have a conversation with Frank. She completed her routine checkup in less than fifteen minutes and found no anomalies, nothing to suggest anything odd was occurring with the old man. Surely, nothing like what Frank had described before she entered.

Turning around, she found Frank standing near the living room's large window. The afternoon light poured through it behind him, and bands of sweat shone on his wrinkled brow.

His weary eyes pleaded with need, anticipation etched on his face as he watched her approach.

His hands slowly lifted from his denim pockets, and he held them out sideways near his chest, palms up. While in the act, he asked, "Did you see anything? Anything like we discussed?" His words were weak, tentative.

Her strides ended near the window, feeling the sun's radiant heat flow through the glass. Her eyes slipped to the carpet momentarily before latching onto Frank again, biting her bottom lip. She exhaled deeply before answering, "Frank, I've been with the company for sixteen years. I've seen thousands of patients just like your father. Every single one left a lasting impression on my heart, but no two patients are alike." She paused, staring into Frank's eyes, empathy spiraling through her core.

"With advanced age, their bodies and minds deteriorate, and we start to see strange things. We *hear* strange things, as well, but it's perfectly common. The mind is an amazing organ, but it only functions for a period, Frank; it has a shelf life, per se."

Frank leaned forward, uncertainty swimming in his features. "So, did you see it? His eyes and the whispers. The hiss? You heard it?"

That calming smile returned to her lips. "We spoke briefly—in between your father drifting in and out of slumber. Coherence eluded his speech, though. Mumbles and grunts mostly. This is very normal. The few times he glanced toward my voice, his eyes were normal for a man in his condition: glossy and shaky. A man living with this disease."

Frank stiffened. "His eyes were fine? Are you sure? Maybe you couldn't really see because of the light."

"What I saw was a man at peace. A man at the end of his life, Frank." She paused, letting the words settle in before continuing. "There's nothing to worry about here. And I'm sure it was a full life, given that *you* are here. This can't be easy, but bringing him to your home to live out his final days, it's clear how much you love your father."

The words rushed in like a tidal wave, dousing him in emotions. This life-changing decision came to him abruptly just hours ago, and it lacked an ounce of selfishness. He found pride in that, but his mind also meandered to the past, pondering those dark years of detest. For as long as he could remember, he blamed his father for his shortcomings: his life choices, his addiction, his arrest. But somehow, seeing his father dwindle down to a brittle shell whisked away the lingering anger suppressed below the surface.

Frank's rigid stance softened. "So, what I described is . . . normal?"

"I wouldn't say the 'eyes' thing is normal, but I have experienced similar events with past patients. Like I said, Frank, at this stage, your father is losing control of his cognitive abilities and motor functions. Muscle control being the most common. Sometimes strokes."

Frank cupped his chin with his hand, listening to her speak. His ignorance on the subject showed, and he felt small, petty, but it also brought relief. "Do you think I'll see it again?"

She shrugged. "Maybe, but remember, it's a part of the journey. All you can do is be here for him and help him navigate." She reached out and patted his forearm. "Try not to put too much stock in what you saw. I can tell it shook you, but there's nothing to worry about. He's just an old man at the end of his rope."

"And that sound. The hiss? The whispers?"

"I'm pretty sure that falls under the same umbrella, Frank. You'll hear sounds, see things, but don't let them deter you. That's your father in there, and you are helping him move on from the tangible world. You're his guide."

Frank stood there contemplating the moment, thinking about Emma's words and the future. He knew from the start this wouldn't be easy, and her soft, comforting voice soothed his tension, but something still itched at his skull's base, festering and scratching. He was grateful for her time and expertise, but something still felt off. Something he couldn't put his finger on.

"Thank you for the kind words. Emma. Hopefully, I can be that person and fulfill that role." His forced grin faded into a thin line while he stared past her black frames. *But honestly, I have my doubts,* he thought.

From within her purse came a startling ring; both jerked at the sudden sound.

"Holy mother-of-pearl." Emma clutched her chest before pulling the bag off her shoulder. She opened the bindings and fiddled through the contents. "That scared the bejeezus out of me." Seconds later, she removed a small, black iPhone, holding it to her face. The screen lit up, illuminating her face, reading the caller's name. "It's the office, Frank. I have to take this," she stated, holding up an index finger. "My work's never done, you know."

"I'm sure it's not, Emma. I'm sure it's not." Frank watched as she turned from him and strolled toward the front door, accepting the call in mid-stride before stepping out onto the front porch. "Take your time."

The quiet conversation from outside was low and muffled. Frank didn't want to invade her privacy by listening in, so he went back to the bedroom. Cautiously, he twisted the knob and leaned through the door's opening. Through the dimness, he could see his father lying in bed, propped up by pillows and fast asleep. A gentle, peaceful snore escaped from deep in the man's throat.

Knowing everything was fine, he stepped into the room.

Minutes later, Frank's eyes darted to the jarred bedroom door, hearing a subtle knock. He sat in a foldable steel chair next to the hospital bed. Just outside the doorframe was Emma, peering through the jamb, still wearing her warming smile.

"Frank, I have to go see another patient. Quite a few on my docket today, but I'll be back tomorrow evening to check in." She spoke with a gentle, hushed tone, her words barely reaching the ears of those around her.

"Yeah, okay. I understand." He lifted himself from the chair, making his way forward toward the doorway. He attempted to match her smile, forcing it. "Let me walk you out."

3

"Shit, Pops. Try to get some of this in your mouth." Frank held a vanilla yogurt, shoveling a spoonful toward his father's waiting mouth. The old man smacked his lips, a mess in the making.

What the hell are you doing, man? You were fine this morning. You act like you've never eaten before. Frank shook his head, amused by the sight.

"No, close and swallow. Like this." He mimicked the actions, Adam's apple bobbing. "There you go. That's better. " Frank set the empty container down on the chair before wiping his father's lips with a napkin. This was the first time he had gotten his father to eat since arriving earlier in the day. The task wasn't easy, yet he didn't mind it, surprisingly.

With the soiled napkin in one hand, he picked up the yogurt container with his free hand. "I'm going to throw these out, okay?" He leaned down over the bed, tapping his father's forearm. "I'll be right back."

Frank's father gazed up from the bed's comforts, wariness dancing across his face. Mumbles trembled from his parched lips as he felt his son's touch fade.

"Just going to the kitchen. Two minutes, okay?" With that, Frank exited the bedroom, aiming for the pathetic excuse of a kitchen. Hardly room for more than a stove and refrigerator, but it served its purpose. Minimal cabinets adorned the wall, and a square wooden table and chairs rested in the corner. Outdated yellow and teal tiles encrusted the counter and backsplash. A single slim window rested above the sink, protected by a series of vertical bars affixed to the exterior.

Frank stopped at the trash can, stepping on the pedal to open the lid. He dropped the remains of his father's meal inside without a second thought before approaching the sink. The bar of soap he scooped up held the previous day's work: grime and grease from towing, but he couldn't care less. Like anything, it would all wash away.

The steady stream of water echoed against the porcelain, filling his ears. It was soothing, almost hypnotic. He stopped the feverish scrubbing and followed the sound, spiraling around and around into the dark depths of the drain. So black. So void. It seemed to have no ending, and it felt like he was plummeting. Falling through time and space with nothing but darkness enveloping his body. Utterly alone.

He stood there for several seconds, a slight sway in his stance. A shudder crept up his spine as he regained focus. He ignored the towel hung around the metal bar near his waistline, choosing to wipe the remnants of hydration across his face. His mind felt drained and maybe this would deliver a burst, some much-needed energy. He closed his eyes, feeling the cool water penetrate his skin, his thoughts. The act was cleansing, but it also reignited a memory from long ago. The night his brother Mikey died.

4

Nearly eight years had passed. Eight long years, but time doesn't heal loss. The mind moves forward, preoccupied by stress and masked by the ambiguities of daily life, yet the pain lingers. It settles just below the surface, hiding and waiting, but every once in a while, it burrows from its hole.

Michael Collins, more affectionately known as Mikey, was an idol to his younger brother. From the moment Frank took his first steps, he clung to him like a shadow, following him wherever he went: the bathroom, the garage, the backyard. He was always there, yearning for the attention all younger siblings seek. Pestering like a buzzing gnat.

The affection wasn't reciprocated in the early years, probably because of the age gap of nineteen months, but over time, Michael accepted his brother and the two became inseparable. Best friends.

They grew up in your common '80s household. Three bedrooms and two baths. Their father was the breadwinner, earning a respectable salary from Union Pacific Railroad. The job was demanding, siphoning his time and attention, but he loved raking in the money, which helped support the family, among his other interests.

The boy's mother, Lynda, was your classic homemaker. Laundry, cleaning, and cooking controlled her days, but she enjoyed the role. That and caring for her sons. She packed their lunches, walked them to the bus stop, patiently waited for their return after school.

She worked hard keeping the house tidy and organized, clean, which isn't an easy feat with two growing boys running around. She rarely took a second for herself, except for the hour she took off to watch *Days of Our Lives*—noon to one, like clockwork. Other than that, her time, love, and devotion were aimed at her family.

That all changed one day in the early '90s. In fact, everything changed after the phone call.

Fourteen years. Fourteen years and two beautiful sons. Their life, their trust, their family. All of it shattered in an instance by another woman's voice.

Lynda always knew the boy's father had a wandering eye, a flirtatious appetite: waitresses, bank tellers, innocent banter between the sexes. She grew used to it, knowing it was just a part of his charm, that same charm that had won her over years before. Harmless acts by her tall, handsome knight in shining armor. She scoffed at the idea he'd ever betray her. They were happy.

Within a week of discovering the affair, and that Frank, Sr. had an infant daughter, she packed a bag and left, moving to her mother's place in Oregon.

The abandonment shuddered through the house. The boys were lost, but at least they still had each other to rely on. Their father, though, wallowed in a pit of misery. Slowly, he drowned himself in booze, rinsing away the guilt with each sip. Before he knew it, he had lost his job along with his wife. Rock bottom.

While Frank, Sr. swirled in despair and self-loathing, the boys discovered new independence. There were no checks, no balances, no rules in the house. They were free to come and go as they pleased, running the streets, getting into mischief, fights. Petty crimes followed, along with their first taste of experimentation.

Following in their father's indulging footsteps, the two started stealing beers from the refrigerator, shotgunning them in the backyard. Michael, being the older, more *responsible* of the two, always instigated the sessions, daring Frank to slam his cold one in less time. Of course, Frank, Sr. caught wind of the theft, seeing his case of Natural Ice deteriorate faster than normal. Through the onslaught of verbal accusations and occasional backhands, the boys persevered. They stuck together, holding their own against his rage. The wedge widened.

By the time the boys reached high school, more exhilarating substances flowed through their bloodstream. Weed, mushrooms, and acid being the common assailants. Coke came later. The euphoric highs took them to levels and places they never imagined. They were hooked, and they loved it.

Neither graduated, and at the time, neither gave a rat's ass. An abusive, drunken father loomed in the household, and they hadn't heard or seen their mother in years. The next hit was their only mission, their only purpose. And finally, it broke their fraternal chain.

The night it happened, heavy drops fell from the heavens, painting the streets. Frank and Michael sat in a late '90s Camry parked in an alley downtown, listening to the rain splatter against the windshield. The car ran, but they had killed the headlights after parking. Their one friend who owned a working vehicle loaned it to them under a certain condition: he'd receive a cut of the score. The two waited, fidgeting in their seats, feeling the onslaught of withdrawal trickle in. They'd been here before, but they'd never bought from Carlos. They'd never even met him. He was new to the scene, earning quite a reputation, and the sample the two savored was grade A: succulent and mouthwatering. Heroin was their new candy, and this was an invitation to the party.

Through the darkness and rain, neither saw the gunman coming. Before Frank could blink, the passenger side window exploded in an echoing bright blast. Shards of glass and crimson littered the cab, blinding Frank, while a sudden jolt of pain pulsed in his shoulder. Through the shock and turmoil, he grasped the scene. Michael leaned his way, hunched forward toward the dash. A stream of blood dripped from his head, pooling onto the cheap rubber mat below. Three bullets had penetrated his temple, and the fourth struck Frank. The assailant fled without a word.

Hours later, the police interviewed Frank in the hospital, asking questions that were wrapped in accusation. Judgmental eyes hovered over his tracked arms with each inquiry. He and his brother were low-time burnouts, and neither detective nor patrolman bought the bullshit he fed them. He didn't know if Carlos ordered the hit, but it was an easy way to make a name for himself. Taking out a scumbag just for the sake of it. It would make others wary about crossing him, and no one outside of their small circle would miss Mikey.

Frank could have given Carlos up, but he knew that saying the man's name would be lethal. Enough bloodshed had occurred. And even though the pain hadn't settled in yet, his brother was gone. He also recently discovered he was going to be a father.

Frank stood in the kitchen, eyes closed, thinking about that night. The rain and darkness surrounded him, entombing his thoughts. He could see the drops striking the windows, splattering like fragments of shrapnel before pooling away. The loamy, gritty scent of the alley penetrated his nose. The memory felt so real.

Eminem's "Lose Yourself" softly bumped from the speakers, matching the rhythmic pattern of the downpour. Frank glanced around the cab, remembering every finite detail. To his right was Michael, a black hoodie pulled over his head, masking his features. Slowly, his brother's neck turned to face him, but only darkness lingered within the hood. He couldn't see an inch of skin, merely blackness pulsing with organic traits.

Frank leaned forward, squinting his eyes. *Mikey?*

The music and the patter of rain faded away, leaving the memory in utter silence. The dark substance filling the hood writhed and squirmed. Appendages oozed from the opening, gripping the sides of the fabric like serpentine fingers, wriggling their way out.

What the fuck is this? This isn't what happened. This isn't real.

Shock held firm like a gauntlet, forcing Frank to watch. Within heartbeats, the material covered Michael's frame, the passenger seat, the dash, the roof. Like a decaying virus, it flowed freely and painted the cab's interior. It crept in from every direction, imprisoning Frank. And there was nothing he could do but wait for it to devour him.

But suddenly, the sleek, fluid like material stopped. Pinned against the window, Frank watched as a thick tentacle emerged from the mass, twisting and stretching toward him. The rounded tip slowly morphed and flattened inches away from his face. Nostrils, eye sockets, and a thin slit resembling a mouth formed. From deep within the sunken orbital depressions, a soft glow emerged, a subtle white before changing to a dull yellow. They were eyes. But the arrangement was wrong. The pupils were wide, horizontal like a goat's.

All around him, the pulsing material stiffened like black ice, but Frank couldn't break his gaze. Seconds later, the slit parted, and a slithering voice filled the silence.

"*Franky.*" The name dripped with desire. "*Your flesh shimmers like a sow's swollen teat.*"

A gasp sprang from Frank, and he flailed away from the sink, landing on the floor. His eyes twitched, taking in the dingy kitchen, the cupboards, the counter. In the background, the sound of running water pounded his ears. "The hell just happened?" he mumbled.

As his pulse slowed, he lifted himself back up and stepped forward toward the sink. With a twist, the running water stopped. He stared into the drain, watching the final beads flow away into the abyss.

His head shuddered with each step as he approached the bedroom, not understanding the memory, the haunting vision. It all seemed so real.

He entered the bedroom, cautious of footfalls. He hoped his father had passed into slumber. The day had been taxing, and he needed some rest. A few hours to recoup, refresh. His eyes strayed to the hospital bed. His father lay there, motionless. The familiar snore was faint and distant.

He eased onto his mattress positioned in the corner, closing his tired eyes. He hoped for some peace, but the vision from his memory looped in his mind. And the worst part was the agonizing sound that followed the vision. The voice. It terrorized his mind until the darkness took control and he joined his father deep in sleep.

4

Shadows

Shadows pushed forward, testing their courage, lapping at his flesh with forked tongues. With each advance, soft whispers leaked in his ear, urging him, steering him. "Just a little further, Franky."

He sat on the pavement, his back pressed against a brick building. He could feel the serum coursing through his blood, raging like a wildfire. It felt magnificent—the euphoria, the freedom, the bliss. It was unlike anything he'd experienced before.

Dropping the syringe, his eyes followed the spiraling hues drifting through the air. With a limp arm, he reached for the myriad of colors dancing before him. Loose fingers playfully jostled the deceptive scene, disturbing the image like a stone tossed into a still pond. A droopy smile crossed his lips as he watched the vibrant tints meld into one.

Fixated by the beauty, he didn't notice the shadows surrounding him. They blanketed the alleyway behind, filling it with the scent of corrosion and misery. Their pulse-like beat devoured his inhibitions, guiding him deeper into the depths of self-affliction.

Incoherently, he lifted himself from the grime, unaware of the puppet master's strings. He staggered through the space, chasing the taunting lights and whispers. Rounding a corner, he paused, leaning against a dumpster. A familiar, animated voice penetrated his thoughts.

Franky. Keep going.

His pace increased as he followed the illusions through the labyrinthian maze. The cancerous shadows crept along just behind him, matching his stride. As they covered brick, plaster, glass, and wood, maggots and boiling tar loitered, leaving trails of decay in their wake.

Through the glamorous display of light, a lone silhouette materialized in the distance. He paused mid-stride, palm pressed against a wall of cinder blocks. His dilated eyes attempted to steady on the subject. After achieving minimal focus, he could see that a woman stood in the alley's center. Long auburn hair loosely swayed with the gentle afternoon breeze, but she was too far away to distinguish whether or not he knew her.

He squinted, glaring through the kaleidoscope of shifting patterns. With a limp hand, he fanned at the lights, sweeping them across the scene. They scattered and dissolved, leaving a hazy view of the mystery before him. Her features seemed familiar, and her presence alone elevated his ecstatic state.

There she is, Franky. Go to her. She needs you.

Frank could feel his body dragging forward, but his limbs never reacted to the motion. Through levitation or another unworldly means, he approached this enigma, this woman.

Inch by inch, the muddled scene cleared, revealing the woman's identity. At least an unfeasible form of it.

Chloe?

The nose, the eyebrows, that slick grin she sported. The purple nevus—an angel's kiss—just under her jawline. It was his daughter, only older, now in her early twenties.

"Chloe. What's happening?" His voice choked as he took in the young woman. "Baby, what is this? Why do you look so mature? Where are we?" The fluidity of his involuntary advance slowed as he drew nearer to her. He stared at her for several seconds as love filled his heart, rinsing away the toxins.

She took a step forward, sincerity shedding off each lucid gesture. "Everything's okay, Daddy. You've found me. I'm really here."

"But how are you . . . so old? This isn't possible. You're only eight, baby."

She ignored the question. "I've been waiting for you. Waiting so long." Her eyes sparkled against the midday sun. "Why did it take you so long?"

"Oh, baby. I'm sorry. It's been too long for any father and daughter to be apart. Life's been shit, but I'm here now."

"I've been alone, Daddy." The warmness of her presence suddenly cooled. "Alone for so long."

His heart skipped a beat, shattering like ice. He pushed forward, taking her hands into his. "Baby, I've tried so hard to get you back. The courts, the legal fees. I swear to you I've tried."

As he pleaded, her stance stiffened, and the soft, soothing grin faded into a displeased line.

"Chloe, I swear. I've been working so hard toward this." He could feel her hands pulling away. "These things don't happen overnight."

Silence ensued as he watched her retreat, arms crossing over her chest.

"Chloe? Baby, I'm doing everything I can. You have to—"

Slender fingers slid across the top of his shoulders, cutting him off mid-sentence. "You're too late, Franky. She's mine."

The whisper lapped at his lobe, and he spun around. The only thing his eyes could reveal was bubbling rot, while wisps of steam rose from the sodden ashes. As his sight fluttered to the heavens, a scorched sky became reality. Clouds of fire and magma dominated the horizon, devouring any remnants of life.

Then the smell struck him like a mule's kick: sulfur, death, and burning flesh. Buckling over, Frank retched and coughed, gasping for an ounce of clean air. With palms pivoting on his knees, he convulsed, straining to empty his stomach's contents. A mirrorlike black substance spewed from his gaped mouth, splattering on the ground like a hailstorm.

As the straining waned, his watery vision refocused. Blood dripped from his nose as he stared at the mess, splattering amongst the heap of black goo. There, in the middle of the dark spew, a newborn formed. A premature, defenseless little girl, no longer than a ruler. A severed umbilical cord jutted from her belly, lying in the heap of black vomit.

Confusion strangled his mind, but he knelt down, taking in the sight. She was alive, faint coos and babbling departing her pursed lips. Without care, he swooped the fragile bundle up, cradling it in his arms. She was weightless, barely noticeable in his brawny grip. He studied her, covering every inch of innocence. That's when he saw it—the birthmark. The same apple-shaped blemish Chloe had under her chin.

As the chaos and inexplicability rushed in, his eyes betrayed him. The little girl, *his* little girl, morphed into something unimaginable. There, in his rough, overworked hands, writhed a pulpous, black slug. The creature squirmed and lurched back and forth, covering his palms in gelatinous soot. Instinctively, he pulled his hands away, allowing the wriggling mass to fall to the ground. As it struck, the matter melted away, joining the congealing pool of ash.

He staggered backward, wiping his hands on his thighs.

"*She's mine, Franky.*" The voice echoed from behind him, forcing a flinch. He felt his body freeze like a block of ice. "*We've had our fun, but you bore me.*"

Jaw agape, he slowly looked over his shoulder. The older version of Chloe stood there once again, head cocked to the side. Everything about her had changed; her stance had become aggressive, the soft grin replaced by a glaring sneer. As he completed the turn, she lifted her arms out to the side, exposing and flexing elongated fingers adorned with surgical-like talons on each tip. And her eyes—black as night and lifeless.

As she rolled her shoulders, Frank could hear each tendon, vertebra, and bone crack in a sequence of rhythmic terror. Once the act was complete, a sinful, satisfied smile reestablished its position on her lips. And behind that beam of horror was an abomination; rows of razor-sharp canines protruded from her vibrating mouth. Streams of saliva dripped from every tooth as she locked onto her prey.

The last vision to synapse in his mind was his daughter, Chloe, leaping at him and crunching down on his skull.

2

Frank sat up in a gasping rage of despair, arms guarding his face and head. His heart pounded in his chest. Buckets of sweat soiled the ruffled sheets around him. Through the dim light, he stared around the bedroom, trying to catch his breath. His father's hospital bed came into view. A dream. A tormenting, terrible dream.

With a sigh, he lowered his body back onto the mattress, mind splintered. As he adjusted his pillow, his stare landed on the ceiling. He lay there for several minutes, fingers locked behind his head, listening to the subtle sounds around him. The floor fan's blades, the familiar faint snore of his father across the way.

His mind wandered, thinking about the dream, about Chloe.

What the hell was that? Why did she look like that? Does she think I haven't tried to get her back?

These thoughts grounded his skull, burdening the self-imposed idea that he had done everything he could to get her back. Could he have done more? Did he deserve to have her in his life? The thoughts looped. Even if he tried, sleep had escaped him.

Shortly after his arrest, the county placed Chloe in foster care. The authorities first entertained the thought of placing her with Frank's father, but they quickly swept it under the rug, citing his advanced age and newly established diagnosis. He was in no shape to care for a young child. With no family in the city besides the old man, she became a ward of the state, bouncing around between families. Frank hated the thought of her living under another's roof, but he also realized how badly he had fucked up.

Wide awake, he brushed the sheets away and swung his legs off the mattress. He sat there for a moment, brewing over the dream, his daughter. His toes wiggled in the shag carpet covering the floor. He scratched the back of his head before standing and exiting the room without making a sound.

After relieving himself in the bathroom, he stared at his reflection in the mirror. For as long as he could recall, those dark circles under his eyes lived there, jabbing at him, reminding him of his unhealthy past. He leaned forward, seeing how they seemed a deeper tint, more prominent. With the red hues suffocating his sclera and his week-old shave, he looked like shit. Shaking his head, he strolled into the front room, collapsing into the recliner.

A digital clock sat on a cheap, three-legged wooden table next to the chair. The glowing digits read 4:27, highlighting the tabletop in a tint of green. Against his better judgment, he picked up his cell phone lying next to it. He paused for a second, thinking about the time, wondering how she would react to the early morning call. Yet he needed to speak to someone, and Damaris was always there for him.

The girl next door was how he viewed her. When he first moved into these low-income apartments, Damaris found him. With a gleaming smile, she offered to help him with the few clusters of boxes he brought. He tried to brush off the advance, but her persistence leaked like an open wound. She even helped him carry the sagging mattress and chair inside. A genuine act by a genuine person. He liked her giddy laugh and hippieish looks. There was an attractiveness there, and he enjoyed her company.

As the days went on, he discovered they shared similar histories and pain. She was an ex-junkie, too, divorced, and had a son. But the boy lived with his father up in Fresno, and she hadn't seen him in a year. She lost all parental rights, along with their relationship, during her last relapse. He also learned about her methadone addiction now that she was off the good shit. Pity struck him, but he was in a similar boat. Before he realized it, he had a best friend.

Besides the few random hookups in the beginning, their relationship remained platonic. They both agreed it was for the best, even though she was the first he had since his release. Since Claudia. He didn't need the weight of a relationship, not with the memories of Claudia festering in his mind, her dead stare glaring his way. They were just good friends who could lean on each other when needed. And he needed her now.

Damaris was a light sleeper, and she could bring some grumpiness with her when disturbed. Frank's thumb hovered over the <**CALL**> button, again considering the early morning time. Weighing the odds, he pressed it.

On the third ring, a groggy voice came through the phone's speaker.

"What the fuck's going on, Frank? What time is it?" He could hear the annoyance loitering in her throat.

"Hey, Mari. Sorry about that." He sat up in the chair, choosing his words. "It's uh . . . it's just after four."

A raspy cough rattled through the phone, followed by the flint of a lighter striking. After pulling in a deep breath and an equally long exhale, she countered his claim. "Half past four in the morning! What the hell, man?"

"I know. I know, Mari. It's early, but I needed to talk to someone. Talk to you."

"Frank, it's the middle of the night. I texted your dumb ass hours ago."

He glanced over at the clock, considering ending the call. But he was already knee-deep in the shit. "Yeah. Yeah, I know. I saw the message. I'm sorry I didn't get back to you earlier. Something . . . kind of come up."

Another inhale and exhale sounded in his ear. "Sure seems that way. Who's the old man?"

A faint chuckle crept from his lips. "Yeah, I had a feeling you'd noticed that. Always on watch, huh?"

"Someone has to be with all the shit that goes down around here. Besides, you live like twenty feet away, and our front doors face each other." She paused and he could hear bed sheets shuffling. "It's hard to not notice something in this place."

Grinning, he swiveled in the recliner, turning and staring out the large window toward her apartment. Hard water stains peppered its lower left side. "That's true."

"You didn't answer my question, Frank. Is that old man your dad?" A yawn muffled the last few words.

"Yeah, sure is." He noticed the light in her hallway switch on. "He's here. Going to stay with me for a while."

"Didn't you say he was in the hospital? What's he doing there with you?"

"It's kind of a long story, Mari." Through the window, he could see her staggering down the hall and entering the bathroom, hair disheveled and covering her face. "One I'll share soon, okay?"

Another yawn poured through the phone. "Well, I'm awake now, asshole. I'm all ears. What's really going on, Frank? What do you need to talk about?"

He sighed, mind volleying between the dream and his father. "I . . . I kinda need your help."

"Okayyyy." The second syllable stretched out like an accordion. "What do you need help with, man? What's this about?"

He adjusted in the chair, choosing his words. "Mari, I need your help with something. I just had this crazy-ass dream about my daughter. You remember Chloe, right?"

"Yeah, sure. You've mentioned her a few times."

He sighed. "Well . . . shit, how do I say this? It was fucking weird. She was older, like way older. And she hated me. It was like she thought I hadn't tried to find her, get her back."

"She was older?" The sound of a toilet flushing sounded in his ear. "That is weird. Where did that come from, you think?"

He shook his head, wondering the same. "Couldn't tell you, but it was so vivid and it seemed so real, Mari."

"Most dreams that have meaning usually do." Her voice faded, and there was a pause while Frank listened to running water before she continued. "You dreamt this for a reason, and now you need to figure out why."

He considered the comment for a moment before responding, "What do you mean, Mari?"

"Come on, man. Our dreams connect us to our consciousness. There is always a link between the dreamworld and our physical realm. Even though they seem abstract and fucking weird, there's a deeper understanding if you unravel the thread. Think about it. Why'd she look older? What did she do that made you think she hated you?"

Chewing on his lip, he thought about her words, her questions. He knew the answers, though. It was guilt. He could feel it creeping up from his stomach's pit. His parental track record lacked merit. He was always high as a kite or belligerent when he had Chloe. The addiction took her from him, and he let it happen. He was a shitty father. Chloe's situation was his fault. He acknowledged that a few weeks after his withdrawal symptoms ended.

"I think I'm worried she'll grow up without me and that I'll never get her back." His eyes caught the bathroom light switch off, and he could see her frame shuffling toward the front room. "She'll resent me for it. Hate me for abandoning her, for leaving her. That's why I dreamt about her in that manner."

He could see Mari collapsed in her chair. Her stare aimed through the glass window facing Frank's apartment. "Yeah, I know how you feel, man. You know, guilt is a lot like a parasite, Frank. It feeds and feeds and feeds until its host can't go on. It doesn't have morals or follow any rules of ethics. It will devour you if you let it." She started twirling a wisp of her long, wavy hair around her finger. "Don't let it consume you, Frank."

"I know. I know." He released an exhaustive sigh. "It's fucking hard, though."

"Hey, as long as you are doing your part, everything's going to work out. Remember what Bob always said?" She started singing the chorus in a bad Jamaican accent, "Everything's gonna be all right."

This forced a chuckle, and Frank buried the ill thoughts, feeling a smile creep across his lips. "Thanks, Mari. I needed that. I really appreciate you."

"No worries. I'm always here for you, man."

"Hey, I'm glad you mentioned that because I do need something from you. A favor. Do you think you could come over in a few hours and hang out? Watch after my old man. I need to get down to Social Services and find out what's happening with my daughter."

A moment of silence followed before she responded, "I don't know, Frank." She stirred in her chair. "Like, what would I have to do? Feed him? Change him?"

"Yeah, he needs both." He leaned forward, hoping she could see him, see the need in his eyes.

She hesitated again. "It's Saturday, man. My day to lounge and be free. Besides, I suck at caregiving. Never any good at it.

"It won't be all day, Mari. And you probably won't have to do much. Just check on him every once in a while. Maybe sit with him, talk to him."

Now it was Mari releasing a winded sigh. "How long are we talking, man? A few hours? I'm not good with old people."

"A few hours, tops. I promise. I just need to get some answers and I can't do that over the phone. Every time I call them, it just rings and rings." He rolled his shoulders, feeling the nerves racing back in. "Please, Mari. From one friend to another. I need this small favor."

He watched as she brought a faint flame toward her waiting lips, lighting a cigarette. The glow accentuated her tired face for a moment. After the initial inhale, bellows of smoke escaped each nostril before slowly floating away like a dissipating cloud.

"All right, man. I'll be there around seven, okay?"

"Thank you. Thank you, Mari. This means a lot."

"I know." These were the last two words she said before ending the call. She sat there for several moments, never averting her stare, taking long drags off her cigarette before extinguishing it. With the nicotine pumping, she stood and shuffled away down the hall, disappearing into the dark cavity of her bedroom.

5

DAY DREAMS

HIS KNUCKLES WHITENED FROM the grip, feeling the streams of rage flow through his veins. No matter how hard he tried, how much effort he brought forth, he was always behind the eight ball. Brushed aside and discarded like a piece of trash. A low-life ex-junkie who can't conform, can't get his shit together, and play out this menacing game we all call life. Maybe it was karma?

His mind looped, thinking about the social worker's words, her absolutism regarding his case. He ground his teeth, thinking about her smug, judgmental expression. Her cheap suit and plastic smile. The artificial empathy pouring from her rehearsed lines. It was sickening.

He had done everything Social Services had asked. He had a job, had proof of residence for over six months, and his piss always tested clean. Yet, it was never enough. Another home visit and drug screen during the following week was the verdict. Followed by a bureaucratic meeting to determine his capabilities of parenthood. Here he was again, driving home in his shitty car, heading toward his shitty apartment, alone, without Chloe. Hoop after hoop.

Once he reached the apartments, he parked the El Camino behind a blue sedan and killed the engine. He didn't exit immediately, though. No, he needed a moment. He needed time to sift through the heap of bullshit.

With his hands still locked at ten and two, he leaned forward, resting his forehead on the steering wheel. He closed his eyes, trying to suppress the anger, the thoughts that continuous rejection weaved. Slow, controlled breaths followed as he tried to steady his pulse. In through the nose, out through the mouth. The act was calming, almost therapeutic. After a few series, the percolation descended back down into his gut.

The exercise eased to a stall, but he remained in the position for several minutes, eyes shut. There was no sound, no motion, nothing to trigger the infernal worry. Just the soothing, blissful peace of the moment. Within his mind, the distress surrounding his life lifted, evincing layers of beauty and hope. He could be patient. He could wait it out for another few weeks. Chloe would be back in his arms, under his roof, before the moon's turn.

A vision of his eight-year-old daughter bloomed within his thoughts, clad in her infamous purple hoodie she used to wear. She ran through an open stretch of grass, arms flailing and pigtails whipping in the breeze. Innocent laughter sprang from her, and the warm clatter wrenched his heart. Her happiness was all he cared about.

The vision pulled him along, watching his little girl's sporadic cartwheels and exuberant play. This is how he remembered her: full of life, pure, and carefree.

As her manifestation ventured further, saplings and shrubs emerged, ending the vast openness. She weaved between the vegetation, giggling with each turn, glancing backward at him, a contagious smile aimed his way.

He followed closely, watching as she dipped and hid behind the obstructions before running off to find a new hiding spot. Titter filled the air, echoing around him, in between her playful calls, "Daddy, Daddy, come find me."

He pushed forward, easing through the thickened space, brushing past mature trees. Glimpses of Chloe flickered between the onslaught of foliage and bark, but her calls remained. "Come on, Daddy. Hurry."

His pace quickened, stepping over foot-tall thickets and bushes. In every direction his eyes danced, towering trees obstructed his view, snuffing the brilliance of the sun overhead. The forest enclosed, trapping him in a strangling grip of branches and thorns, and he lost sight of her. Squeezing between two trunks, he felt the rigid bark tearing at his flesh. "Chloe! Baby, come back!"

She didn't respond, but he could still hear her playful laughter lingering in the loamy forest. He writhed and clawed at the branches, trying to pull himself along, but he could move no farther. He was stuck, immobilized. "Chloe!"

The remaining sliver of light drained from the sky and darkness bullied forward, approaching from every angle. Within its presence, Frank could feel a wave of scorching heat as his forehead beaded up. And he didn't feel alone. Someone or something was with him, lurking and watching.

A tapping sounded on the driver's side window brought him spiraling back to reality. Flinching at the sound, his hand inadvertently slammed on the car's horn while scooting toward the seat's center. With ragged breath and adrenaline pumping, his eyes shot to the source. Just outside the car was a woman wearing forest green scrubs. She leaned down, peering into the car's cab while wearing a familiar smile. It was Emma.

2

Seconds later, Frank flushed the nerves away and collected himself, exiting the car with haste. His fluttering heart skipped while he stood there, trying to conceal the dwindling shakes in his fingertips. This new vision left him reeling, wondering if he was going mad, wondering why these ill thoughts of his daughter plagued his mind.

With a forced grin, he greeted the hospice nurse, "Uh, hey there, Emma. Sorry, you startled me. I was just . . . just trying to take a second to think."

Warmth radiated from her stare as she watched him, concern coated with a layer of empathy. Past her glasses' black frames, her light brown eyes sparkled. "Hey there back, just Frank. We all deserve moments now and then." She raised her eyebrows. "Miss me?"

"Uh . . . yeah, yeah. Of course." His toothy grin bloomed, feeling the comforts of her presence. He started smoothing out his flannel shirt, unaware of the subtle action. "I didn't expect to see you until later this evening."

"I'm a busy woman, but I make time for all my patients. Besides, I was in the neighborhood and figured I'd come by a smidge early to check on your father."

While his pulse descended, her news filled his ears like music. He still hadn't completely swept the previous day's incident under the rug. He knew his father's condition was dire and that odd occurrences would occur, but that sound . . . It still bothered him. And the damn dreams and visions.

"That's great to hear. I'm really thrilled you're here, Emma." He scratched the side of his face, feeling the day-old stubble.

An awkward silence ensued as they scanned each other, neither sure who should take the lead. Eventually, Frank ineptly gestured toward the house, feeling hues of pink sink into his cheeks.

After a meek nod, Emma rounded the El Camino, stepping onto the sidewalk. As her second Sketcher struck the concrete, she swiveled and turned to face Frank. Under the bright afternoon sun, he could see the faint remains of freckles crossing her cheeks and nose. He hadn't noticed them the day before. They brought a youthful charm.

"You coming, just Frank?"

Feeling a bit like an ass, he dropped his look, shaking his head for a split second.

What the hell is wrong with you, man?

As his stare landed back on her brown eyes, he delivered a similar nod. "Uh, yup." He scurried around the vehicle, closing their distance. Side by side, they strolled up the walkway toward the apartments in silence.

After unlocking the front door, Frank opened it with a grunt, stepping to the side to let Emma pass. Scents of antiseptic and sanitizer wafted toward him as she brushed by. He followed closely, stepping over the threshold and taking in the drab front room.

He noticed his bedroom door was closed, and his neighbor Mari sat in the recliner, cigarette dangling from her slender fingers. She didn't bother to rise or acknowledge their entrance, merely taking in the far wall with an emotionless stare.

Frank shifted, closing the door with strong palms and barring it with the dead bolts. As he turned to face his friend, he called out, "Hey, Mari. Is everything okay? Is my Pops all right?"

Seconds passed before a spark registered in Mari's eyes. She was distant, oddly missing the sloppy, easygoing allure Frank admired.

"Mari? What's wrong? What's going on?"

A flicker of life returned to her face as she registered him, rapid blinks following. "Hey, Frank." But her regular carefree parlance was missing.

Stepping forward, he probed again, concern growing with each subtle stride. "Mari? Did something happen?" His eyes darted to the closed bedroom door.

She didn't answer immediately, but her eyes never left him. "No, no. Of course not. He's just sleeping. He's fine. Who's this?" Her stare landed on Emma, as did his.

"Oh, I'm sorry. Yeah, this is Emma." He backpedaled a step, looking over his shoulder at the nurse standing by the door. "She works for Hospice Care." He gestured toward her with an open hand. "She's here to check on my father."

Mari held her stare as he spoke, taking in the nurse. Nothing lingered in the look, though; it was void, empty.

Feeling a little out of place, Emma chimed in, cutting through the passive tension, "Hi there. Mari, is it?" Her open hand crept forward while approaching the recliner, cautious of being overly friendly. "I'm Emma."

Limply, Mari reached up and grasped her hand, barely looking her in the eyes before releasing it a second later.

As the handshake ended, Mari sighed and peeled her body from the recliner. Her attention shot to Frank, still sporting the deadpan features. "I've got to get home. I need to check on my son." With that, her view flew to the door.

Frank took her in as she shuffled past him. "Of course. I understand, Mari." His erratic mind spun, wondering what the hell was wrong. "Again, thanks for coming over and watching him. This means a lot."

She paused her advance mid-stride, wispy, uncombed hair dangling in her face.

"Hey, I'll text you later. Okay, Mari?"

Stagnant silence. She didn't even bother looking back at him before pushing forward. Seconds later, the front door shut, leaving Frank and Emma alone.

3

Frank entered the bedroom moments later, sitting on his bed's corner, cautious of Emma's purse. The mattress groaned and sagged as his ass sunk into the coils. His eyes hovered over Emma, watching and wondering what she must be thinking. After the confusion with Mari, she left him in the living room without saying a word.

The hospice nurse stood at the foot of the hospital bed. Her nimble fingers massaged and stretched the old man's right leg. This wasn't a common procedure, but inclination presented itself after she saw his face. Discomfort and pain radiated from his every move. Her job was to soothe, to help the man during his final weeks, and she would fulfill that obligation.

"Hey, I'm sorry about that, about Mari. That was very out of character for her. I don't know what happened or what's wrong, but she's usually really friendly."

Emma glanced his way for a split second before returning to her work. "No need for apologies. She seems . . . sweet."

He could taste her sarcasm but declined to open up that jar.

Seconds later, Frank cleared his throat, watching her with his father. "That's really kind of you, Emma."

"Yeah, he needs this. It's important for the limbs to move, for the blood to flow." Without averting her attention, she lowered the right leg and shifted to the left. "Besides, I can already see a change. Color is returning, see?"

He eased from the mattress and strolled her way, staring over the bed's railing. Seeing his father like this was disheartening. For as long as he could remember, his father was a rock, an ox. A stubborn boomer who didn't put up with shit. What his eyes showed him now was a broken, weak man on his deathbed.

"Yeah, I can see it." The statement was a lie; he couldn't see anything but the old man's ashy, frail shins. "He looks better."

She gripped the old man's ankle and slowly rotated it a few degrees. "If I'm not around, make sure you do this at least twice a day. I can tell he appreciates it."

"Oh yeah? How can you tell?"

Her stare fell on Frank while working the joint. "He stopped clenching." She lowered the leg, shifting its direction. "I noticed he was grinding his teeth when I first came in. Usually a sign of agitation."

"Shit. Do you think he's suffering?" He could feel the rush of worry and guilt piling on. "Is there anything else we should do?"

That calm smile returned as she monitored him, noticing his fidgeting manners. "We're doing everything necessary, Frank." With confidence, she reached out and gently placed her palm on his forearm—a comforting embrace. "We just need to be here for him. I know this isn't easy."

He locked onto her, staring past her black frames. "No, no, it's not." His words choked. "I've . . . I've never seen him like this. It's like—"

She cut him off, "Hey, I understand. I do. I've been doing this a long time. It's never easy seeing a parent go through this, Frank. Seeing them slip away."

With welled eyes, he glanced at his resting father. The old man seemed at peace. "It's hard, and I don't understand how it happened so fast." His head dropped, and his posture softened. "He looked bad yesterday, but at least he could communicate. We talked. He didn't know who the hell I was most of the time, but we talked."

Emma found herself nodding while she listened to his rant. She also noticed her light touch on his arm was now a gentle brush. "He said a few words to me yesterday too. Sometimes the regression happens over months. Sometimes it's days. I'm just glad he's here with you and not stuck in a hospital."

He pulled back, ending the closeness between the two. "This doesn't seem right, though." Hints of agitation peppered his speech. "It seems too fast, you know? We played chess yesterday morning, for Christ's sake. Chess."

His helplessness poured from every word, and it crushed her. "Really?" No matter how many families she worked with, the challenge of death never descended, but the idea of this old man playing a cognitive game a day before didn't sit well. "Chess?"

"Yeah, and like he's done my whole life, he kicked my ass and shit-talked the whole time."

Biting her lip, her attention darted to the old man. "Hmm, that is a rapid decline." She stared at Frank's father, ideas and thoughts brewing. "But it does happen."

"Are there any tests or procedures we should do? Anything to help us understand why this happened so fast?" Frustration bloomed in every word.

She turned and took in Frank, seeing the desperation, the need. This was the hardest part of her job. It wasn't the parent or loved one's death. It was the grief of the kin, of the family and friends, on full display. "I wish there were. I really do, but at this stage, being present is the only thing that matters, Frank. Be present and surround him with love and memories. That's what he needs in his final days."

All his life, Frank had never been one to sit around and wait. Patience had always been his foe, but he was out of his league here, lost and overwhelmed by his father, the dreams, the visions. He could feel his mind buckling, and it was on the cusp of breaking.

A long sigh blew from his lips, feeling the sense of defeat settling in. "I just . . . I don't understand how this happened. He's always been so strong, such a hard-ass. And now,"—pausing, he gestured his father's way—"I don't know if I can handle this."

"Hey, no one is wired for this, Frank. This is difficult, life-changing, and you need help." That radiant, warm smile bloomed once more as she neared him. "You're not alone, okay? I'm here."

Staring at her in silence, Frank mulled over her words. For as long as he could remember, at least since his brother's death, he had ridden solo. It was hard to let others enter his ring, but something about this woman convinced him to lower his guard.

He stepped closer, taking in her soft features: the dimples and subtle lines around her eyes and lips. "Thank you, Emma. I don't know what I would do if you hadn't shown up yesterday." He rubbed the top of his shaved head. "On top of everything going on around here, I'm battling Social Services to get my daughter back."

"Oh, wow. *You* have a daughter?" The incredulous words sprang from her lips before she could think. She bit her lip, knowing the words may have wounded him. "I'm sorry, Frank. It's just . . . you never mentioned her before. This is a bit of a surprise."

Frank dismissed the slight. "It's fine. Don't worry about it. Not much of a father figure, right? Besides, how would you have known?"

Intrigue dabbed at her mind, replacing the remorse. "How old is she?"

"She's eight."

"And her name?"

Frank's response lagged. Memories of his daughter rushed in, filling his heart and core. "Her name is Chloe."

Emma's eyes sparkled. "Beautiful. What a beautiful name, Frank. Well, I pray everything works out for you. I hope to meet her someday."

"That would be nice. It really would, but I don't know if that's going to happen." His face slackened, and the warmth deteriorated. "Those bureaucratic assholes keep giving me the runaround. I've done everything they've asked, but it's never enough."

She could see his turmoil, hear the aggravation in his voice. Naturally, empathetic advice populated her mind, but she held her tongue, choosing to let him vent.

"And it's not just Chloe. I've also been having these—" He paused, questioning if he should share this with her: the dreams, the visions. Would she think he was crazy, losing his mind from the stress? Would she label him, judge him? She barely knew him, but something pushed him forward. He didn't feel threatened to reveal some intimate details about his life.

"It's really hard to explain, but I've had these moments where I'm dreaming, and I'm not actually asleep." He lifted his brow, wondering what she was thinking. "It's crazy, I know."

"It's not crazy. We all have moments where we daydream, cut out for a few seconds. It happens all the time. It's normal."

"Yeah, but I've seen some strange things lately. Unexplainable things. And there've been some freaky-ass real dreams too."

"So daydreams and actual dreams. Did they involve your father or Chloe? It would make sense if they did. With everything going on in your life, your mind pinpoints the critical and projects it upon your consciousness. Even if the dream itself is abstract, the focus is on what's happening in your life."

"Yeah, and—" He rubbed the back of his head again, questioning his own sanity. He thought about the dream with Chloe, how old she was, and how she changed. But he also thought about something else. "My brother too."

Emma's eyes widened. "Really? Have you seen your brother recently? Has he been here to help you with your father?"

"No, no. Mikey died years ago. Not a day goes by that I don't think about him, but he's not constantly on my mind. That's why it's so weird."

"I'm sorry to hear that, but that's understandable. Losing a sibling leaves a void in your life, Frank. That's an open wound that will never heal."

"Yeah, I know, but it was how I saw him. That's the weird part, Emma. It was like . . . like something else was there with him, something dark. He changed in the dream, replaced with this dark shit that wasn't him. I don't understand it and it's been eating at me all day."

She nodded, encouraging him to go on without breaking his rhythm. That comfortable, soft glare guiding him.

"And this thing. This black thing that replaced Mikey . . . it spoke. It was so weird, but it said something that still makes my skin crawl."

"Oh, Frank. That must be terrifying. I don't mean to be too forward, but can you share what this dark *thing* said?" That confident grin returned, leading him, peeling back the last few layers of caution. "Maybe there's something hidden in there that we can uncover. You know, together." She winked.

After hesitating for a heartbeat, he dove in headfirst, shedding any lingering threads of worry. "This sounds stupid, and I'm sure it's just my mind screwing with me, but it said, 'Your flesh shimmers like a sow's swollen teat.'"

Silence ensued, stifling the room with uneasiness. Emma's glare seemed to penetrate Frank as she thought about his statement, pondering the meaning and searching for the words to counter.

Frank leaned in, praying he hadn't made a mistake and spooked her. "Crazy, huh? I know how that must sound. It's fuckin' weird. It's really weird, right?"

"That is odd, Frank." She pushed her glasses up the bridge of her nose. "But, are you sure those were the words? The exact words? I know from firsthand experience that we only remember bits and pieces of our dreams. The visuals are usually clear and taxing, but anything else gets fuddled in the haze."

"Oh, I'm sure. That *thing* that was supposed to be Mikey turned and faced me. It said those exact words." A long breath escaped his pursed lips as he watched her closely, eyes searching.

Her eyes shot to the left while she contemplated the response, not sure how to take the affirmation. Eventually, she broke the stillness, glancing at her wristwatch before locking back onto him. "Hey, Frank, I have to get going. I'm already late for my next appointment."

The sudden curve and behavior left him reeling and confused. He had just opened up to this woman, spilling a troubling secret. "Umm, okay. I understand. But any thoughts on what I just said, though? This is really eating at me."

"Yeah, I don't know Frank. Let me chew on it for a bit. We can talk tomorrow." She rushed past him, grabbing her purse from the stacked mattresses Frank called a bed. As she made her way to the door, she paused and turned to face him. "Are you a man of faith, Frank?" She already knew the answer from the slack in his eyes.

Standing there, he stared in her direction, knowing he caused this. By opening up and sharing these dark, intimate experiences, he had driven her away. He had only known her for a few days, but their conversations were so genuine, so real. She felt like an actual friend, something he hadn't really had outside of Mari since his arrest.

He ignored the spiritual inquiry, opting for cordiality instead. "Take care, Emma. And thank you for everything, especially all you've done for my father. I hope to see you tomorrow."

A wan, forced smile crossed her lips before she turned and exited the bedroom. Moments later, Frank could hear the dead bolts unlatched one at a time before the door opened and closed, leaving him alone with his thoughts and new worries. And his sleeping father.

6

MARI

FRANK TOWELED OFF HIS hands, praying the day's work was complete. Hopefully, he could enjoy a few moments of peace and detach from the mundane: the labors, the stresses, his new life. As he rehung the towel, a sense of contentment washed over him, knowing that his father was well-fed and ensconced for the night. The old man even mumbled a slur his way, making him chuckle while he wiped away the remnants of dinner from his frail chin.

As he made his way into the living room, he flopped himself into the sagging recliner. Moments passed while he sat there, staring through the room's large window. The moon's brilliance highlighted the common space outside, and a cricket's soothing rhythm brought amenity.

On the surface, he seemed at peace, justified by the day's outcome. Yet internally, his mind festered. He thought about his daughter, about the damning visions and dreams. He wondered if he'd ever see Emma again, dreading the idea of someone new coming to the house. Would she be that petty and cut ties because of what he said? Have another nurse tend to his father? He wasn't sure, but as he sat there, looking through the water-stained glass, his mind drifted to his neighbor, Mari.

The way she had left earlier this morning pulled at him. Her demeanor was so foreign, so out of character. He knew asking her to watch his father was a big favor, possibly a step or two beyond their friendship line, but it was the only way to get down to the Social Services office. Now, he regretted it and felt the act was selfish.

He dropped his gaze and redirected it at the digital clock sitting on the table next to the chair. It was early by most standards, 8:26. After swiping away the hesitation, he picked up his phone.

The black screen boomed to life, flooding his face with radiance. After adjusting his eyes, he scrolled over the green <**MESSAGES**> button, pressing it with a calloused thumb. The phone wasn't new; he bought it from a street vendor months ago, refurbished, and he had only a few contacts listed. Right on the top was the name he knew he could count on, the name of his only true friend in the world. He pressed her name, *Mari*, and started typing.

Hey, are you awake?

Seconds passed without a response, filling his anxiety. Maybe she was already in bed, perhaps in the shower, or away from her phone, but after his pulse beat a sixth time, the three bubbles appeared next to his message.

Yeah just got out the shower

The word made him realize how badly he needed to bathe.

How was it?

She responded immediately.

Started off great. But I lost heat five minutes in. Ended up freezing my ass off by the time I was finished. Shitty water heater at this pace.

Nodding, his thumbs kept typing.

I know I know. Same thing over here. Everything else ok? You seemed off earlier.

After a few seconds, the three bubbles reappeared but vanished just as fast.

He stared at the screen, impatience building before she began typing again. He watched as the bubbles continued to pulse before a new message, one the size of a small paragraph, appeared on his screen.

Yeah Frank. about that . . . i didn't want to say anything in front of your little friend lol, but something did happen with your dad. you know i'm not good with shit like this taking care of others besides my boy of course. but while i was sitting there in that fart stain you call a chair i thought i heard something from y our room.

He leaned closer, rereading the text and analyzing every word. After the second pass. His thumbs went back to work.

The fuck did you hear? Was he choking or something He does that sometimes Mari

No no. It was something else man. When I opened the door your dad was mumbling and trying to kick his blankets off pissy old thing if you ask me.

Frank's mind raced back to the previous evening, remembering a similar moment.

I've seen that too. And yeah, he can be a real peach. Try living with the SOB for most of your life. Thanks for reminding me

*Mari. Did you hear what he was saying? Is that why you were
acting kinda off*

A minute passed without a response. Tension boiled while
he waited, eyes volleying between the message box and the cute
picture of her in a hippy outfit next to her contact name. He
had taken it the previous Halloween.

As the bubbles reappeared, he loosened his grip on the
phone.

*I walked over to him to calm him down. I fixed his blankets
and then he looked at me. A really weird look, Frank. I don't know
how to say this. He reached up and grabbed my wrist, not hard or
anything, and then he started speaking. but the voice that came
out of his mouth wasn't his.*

Frank froze, reading the message again and again. With a
quickened pulse, he leaped back in.

What does that mean, not his? You've never met him before.

The response was instant.

*I know but what I heard wasn't an old man's voice. The mum-
bles stopped as i stood there listening to him. The voice was clear as
day but . . .*

His thumbs worked feverishly.

But what? What Mari

Slowly, the bubbles appeared once again.

He wasn't speaking english.

His eyes honed in on the message, making sure he hadn't
missed a single word. "Not English. What the hell is she talking
about?" he whispered.

Frank's eyes flew to the window, staring through the glass at Mari's apartment. The tightly drawn curtains in the front room cast a shadowy darkness throughout the space.

Is she fucking with me? he thought.

With the phone in his hand, he escaped the comforts of the recliner and slowly approached the window, eyes fixated. Moments passed while he glared, mind spinning, but the surreal moment ended the second he felt a vibration in his left hand.

Lifting the phone to his face once more, he read her next message, pupils widening.

It kinda freaked me out ya know. Maybe I imagined it or was having some trippy acid flashback. I'm sorry I brought it up. I'm sure it was nothing U have enuf to worry about dude.

His thumbs hovered over the message box, needing confirmation, needing to know more, yet he hesitated. Why was she backpedaling? His mind drifted to the other day when he heard the heinous hiss slither from his old man's lips. As hard as he tried, he couldn't get the sound out of his ears. It was a deafening reminder, coiled and constantly striking.

His eyes darted back to her apartment for a split second before returning to the screen. Seconds passed while he developed the words, caution and worry dueling to the death in his thoughts. Slowly, his response began.

He wasn't speaking english? My pops doesn't know any other languages. You sure

Hey jus forget I brought it up man. I'm sure it was me being crazy, paranoid

He wondered the same about his experience, but deep down, something scratched at his cranium, steering him toward the truth. He knew what he saw and heard, and it wasn't normal.

No mari. Its not your paranoia. I heard something yesterday too. The nurse thinks its apart of his dementia. But i'm not sure I believe that

His heartbeat climbed while he waited, not sure of what to expect next. This day just kept piling on more and more shit, and now he felt like suffocation was looming. Suddenly, his phone rang, and he nearly dropped it to the shag carpet below. With adrenaline spitting into his veins, he pushed the **<ANSWER>** button; it was Mari.

Before he could eke out a syllable, her voice flooded the speaker.

"Meet me outside, man. We need to talk."

2

The crisp, spring air brought a chill to her bare arms, but she ignored it. Her nerves were humming with anxiety as she lit a second cigarette. Smoke billowed from each nostril as she exhaled and spilled her thoughts into the night.

"I swear to you, man. It was a different language, clear as day. Nothing I've ever heard before." She flicked the cigarette, disregarding the ash as it loosely fluttered to the ground. "I didn't want to say anything, get you all riled up, but . . . it was fuckin' weird."

Frank stood facing her on the pathway in between their apartments, hands deep in his pockets. His thick flannel shirt shed the brisk air away, while his attentive mind listened, agreed, but also questioned her words.

With a light shake of his weary head, he replied, "You know the nurse that was here this morning? Emma?" He paused, seeing her nod and a little something else. "Well, she said we would hear some strange things, but this? How could he speak another language? He's never traveled or taken a class. Hell, he's never even been on a plane. He's lived his whole life right here in the shithole we call Bakersfield."

She took a long drag, never taking her eyes off him before continuing. "I'm sorry I didn't tell you this morning, but it shook me up. I just had to get out of there as fast as possible. But I know what I heard, man. It was real."

Frank glanced at his apartment and scratched the side of his face. His mind drifted, reliving that heinous hiss that had sent him reeling. "This is crazy, Mari. All of this is, but I believe you. There has to be an explanation, though. Old men don't just randomly learn new languages."

"I know, I know." She brushed a wisp of wavy hair away from her view, tucking it behind her ear. "But I know what I heard. Like I said, it was something different, foreign maybe. Like those old movies."

Frank cupped his chin, listening to her, hearing the absolution in her voice. Ever since he moved in, Mari had been there, helping him cope, helping him rebuild his life. She was the one constant he could trust and count on, but how could this be real?

"Old movies?" he asked. "Like black-and-white films?"

"Yeah, from over in England or Europe. Swords and chariots and shit. You took some history courses in high school, right?"

A brief chuckle leaped through his teeth. "History? High school? No, not really, Mari. I barely went to school, but it sounds like you did." He scanned her for a brief moment, watching her take another drag. "Bet you really pulled off the Catholic schoolgirl look, huh?" He waggled his eyebrows.

She playfully reached out and slapped his bicep. "Fuck off. I'm serious, man. I don't know what language it was, but it's old, romantic even."

"It just doesn't make sense." He shook his head, clicking his tongue. "How is this possible?"

"I don't fuckin' know, man, but it's real, and it happened. Now, we need to figure out how, and more importantly, why?"

Frank stared at her, his only real friend in the world, the one person he could talk to, share with. After his heart rate calmed, he answered her, "All right. Let's do that." He paused again, biting his lip before continuing. "Would you mind coming inside? Maybe if you're with me, he'll do it again."

3

It took a while to convince Mari to enter his apartment, but she caved to his needs after hearing his poised pleas; his charm could pull her in any direction. He promised nothing would happen, which she knew was true, but she had no control over her hesitation. The episode with the old man clung to her like a leech, draining her mind.

After locking the door, Frank eased toward the bedroom, followed closely by his neighbor and best friend. He paused as they neared, aiming his ear at the bedroom, but all he could hear was the floor fan's sputtering blades circulating to its rhythmic tune. Mari's reluctance bled into his nerves, and his unease was noticeable. As he removed his ear from the door, a smirk crossed his lips, knowing how puerile the act was. What did he expect to hear?

He glanced back at her, making sure the grin had dissolved, and delivered a nod. Meekly, she mimicked the gesture but remained close to him as he turned and grasped the doorknob. As he pushed the door open, he took a single step inside, scanning the room. The lamp in the corner delivered the only faint lighting. He had yet to visit the hardware store and get some new bulbs for the overhead fixture. Everything was in its place, just as they'd left it. Contentment filled the air and not a thing stirred.

He slowly proceeded into the room, feeling Mari wringing the hem of his flannel shirt. Together, they sauntered forward, approaching his father's bed. Once they were within a few feet, their eyes drew to the old man lying on his side, nestled tightly in his blanket. His slumber flushed away any remaining ill thoughts from either of them.

Frank sidled up to the bed's foot railing, watching his father's nostrils flare with each passing breath, but his eyes also picked up on something else while he stood there. An inky blotch blemished the blanket's light gray color near the old man's feet. Frank cocked his head, staring at the anomaly, oval in shape. As he did, he noticed a subtle slow, continuous rise and fall from the thing's center. The looping action mesmerized him, and he could sense himself descending into a trance. His pulse slowed and his breathing relaxed as he spiraled down and down into the depths.

What the fuck . . . he thought, as he leaned in closer.

Suddenly, motion caught his sight, and his view flowed toward the top of the dark shape. A part of the black enigma raised up a few inches, swiveling clockwise toward Frank. The fluidity of the motion was effortless, and it paused once it leveled with his view. Following this act, the unimaginable happened. From the center of the opaque, two yellow orbs appeared, diagonal black slits running vertically through each. And then they vanished within the darkness before returning a split second later.

Frank felt his blood freeze, trepidation locking him in its relentless grip. Seconds dragged along, fueling the dread, and while he stared into the soporific orbs, panic released. But it was too late. He couldn't move, scream, do anything, but melt away.

Behind him, Mari's eyes cast over his shoulder, latching onto the orbs as well, but somehow, she didn't fall into the bottomless pit. She could feel Frank's tension, wondering what the fuss was about. She leaned into him, whispering into his ear, a flush of heat smothering his lobe. "What's up? It's just Max."

As soon as he heard the name, a sudden rinsing showered over him and he realized he had been holding his breath. After glancing sideways back at her, his eyes steadied and focused on the cat lying near his father's feet. Peculiarity washed over him, wondering what had just happened, but like always, he buried it.

"Hey, buddy. Where have you been?"

As he reached down to stroke Max's scruff, the gray tabby recoiled, releasing a cautionary hiss. The animal's needlelike canines shone in the dim light, hinting at their violent potential, and its fur stood on end.

Frank pulled his hand back, watching the aggressive posture and display unfold. "Fuck is wrong with you, Max?" he mumbled, as he watched the cat retreat a few inches, back arched and warnings flinging his way.

He sensed Mari take a step back from behind him, her fingers gradually loosening their hold on his shirt, yet his focus remained locked on the animalistic spectacle unraveling in front of him. "Max, what's wrong?"

Instantly, the animal jumped from the bed, landing on all fours and racing from view like a streak of black. Both Frank and Mari followed the motion, stares aimed at the open door as the animal vanished from sight. A second later, the familiar sound of the flaps from the animal's kitty door echoed through the apartment. With hearts pounding, the two exchanged a wary glance, the lingering tension from the incident palpable between them.

"What the hell's gotten into him?" Mari asked, unable to shake the lingering stress hovering around the room.

"Shit, if I know." Frank's head teetered. "I've never seen him act like that before. He's always been such a lap cat."

"Well, that little demon isn't coming anywhere near my lap for a long time, man. Fuck that cat." Mari shook her head, a cringe stapled to her face.

Frank didn't respond. He couldn't worry about his cat now. Other needs were pressing. His attention leaped back to his father, watching the old man. He shook off the nerves and stepped forward before kneeling to eye level. "Pops? Hey, Pops, can you hear me?" The whispers came out slow, subtle.

The old man's parched lips smacked twice before returning to their soft breaths. His frail, rail-thin body shifted on the mattress, but he couldn't break through the deep slumber.

Frank tried again, getting within a few inches of his father's face. "Pops? Hey, Pops? It's me, Franky. Can you hear me?"

Nothing.

Seconds passed while Frank knelt by the bed, anticipating a reaction but knowing nothing would happen. He studied his father's face, taking in the deep canyons of the man's jowls and the unkempt clusters of hairs protruding from his nostrils and ears. His eyes crept toward the old man, feeling guilt squirm up his throat. He still couldn't understand how this had happened.

While he knelt there, thinking about his father and his child-hood, the old man's eyes sprang open. Frank flinched at the suddenness of the action, locking onto the sight. So many times in his life, he stared into those gray eyes, seeing the fury, the wrath, but the color was missing. His eyes had rolled, and all Frank could see now were the yellowing hues of age and despair. Slowly, the old man lifted his head from the pillow, face tilted toward his son. Despite the gasp that sounded from behind, Frank's gaze remained fixed.

Anxiety percolated, coating the air in a dense layer of grim, but just as quickly as the action developed, it ceased. The old man lowered his head back down into the waiting comforts of the pillow and shut his eyes.

Seconds passed before reality rushed back in. Frank could feel a hand on his shoulder and a soft breath in his ear. "Dude, what the fuck was that?"

Glancing over his shoulder, he caught Mari hovering over him. Her face revealed a look he had never seen, and he imagined mirroring it. "I don't know," he whispered, thinking back over the last few days. " But he's done that a few times. Did it in the hospital too."

"I don't like this, man. I need to leave. Now."

He swiveled, watching Mari backpedal toward the door. But he also noticed her chin and lips. They trembled. "That's fine, Mari."

He stood and stepped in her direction. He had to comfort her, explain that this was just a side effect of the disease. Ease the tension from her mind. But deep within his gut, he knew something was wrong. Something more was happening here. He just couldn't let her know that. "Thanks for trying. Let me walk you out."

As he approached the door, an intense wave of heat struck him, and he stopped mid-stride. With his forehead beading up, his eyes shifted to the left and right, watching the lingering shadows decorating the walls. They seemed to close in on him, advancing in every direction, and faintly, in the back of his mind, he thought he could hear whispers.

Turning around, his eyes landed on his father once more, expecting to see the voidness in the old man's eyes again. But he saw nothing. His father lay there on his side, fast asleep and at peace.

Shaking off the scene, Frank dropped his stare and followed Mari out of the bedroom. As he slowly closed the door, the dim light from the lamp faded, casting the bedroom in complete darkness. With the door slightly ajar, he peered into the opening, wondering when he last changed the bulb. He couldn't recall, but after a few breaths, life slowly reignited the lamp, returning the room to its dimness. He stared at the old lamp in the corner for longer than he knew before his view drifted to his father again. The corners of the old man's mouth curled up, revealing a slight smirk.

Frank dismissed the look and closed the bedroom door.

PART TWO

THE FATHER

7

SOCIAL SERVICES

THE NEXT WEEK AND a half drifted by like a dream, barely nipping the subconscious. Time was a blur, hazed by mundane routine and the appreciated normality of life. The strange, irregular occurrences with Frank's father ceased almost immediately after the incident, ending the ill suspicions. Just a simple cognitive symptom of his condition.

The old man spent his days resting, falling in and out of slumber, occasionally coherent enough to speak to Frank. Nothing made much sense, though. Ramblings from the past, memories of relatives long gone: Lynda, Mikey, other names Frank had no recollection of. It was a bittersweet turn, ending the brooding, but it also allowed mortality to come crawling back into the picture. Frank hated seeing his father in this condition.

The support from hospice continued, too, providing comfort and much-needed help during this difficult time. Skilled, compassionate caregivers stopped by the apartment almost daily, monitoring the old man's status. During the hour or two they were visiting, they would help change his linens or readjust his position to deter any more bed sores from flaring up. But their skill set didn't stop there. They also lent their voice and became a crucial advocate for support. Without the advice and positive thoughts, Frank didn't know what would have happened.

As helpful as they were during this trying time, something was still missing. Emma hadn't returned. With each passing fresh face from the company, Frank would ask about her whereabouts, receiving vague, if not rehearsed, responses. It hurt, knowing he had pushed her away, but like everything in his life, he ignored it.

Mari even returned to the scene after a few days, breaking through the reservations holding her back. She volunteered a fraction of her time to sit with the old man as long as nothing nefarious happened again. And nothing did.

During the days, Frank returned to work while Mari sat in the apartment. It felt good to get out, stretch his legs, shut his mind and emotions off. Collecting the four-wheel debts littered amongst the city helped him regain some clarity. Not to mention the joy it brought. Swooping in undetected and towing away these toys was exhilarating. There was a thrill to it, and it was almost nostalgic.

Every time he hooked up a new Chevy or Ford, a rush doused over him. The same rush he discovered as a youth when his older brother taught him how to shoplift. The threat of being caught, taking the chance, living on the edge. It made him feel untouchable.

And the assholes who couldn't make their payments—these privileged middle-classers, destroying the credit scores without a care—fuck 'em. The masses constantly judged him at every turn, labeling him as a low-life, a bum, a burnt-out addict. He knew he was an outcast. Maybe deep down, towing cars was a way of giving them and the conformity of society the finger.

Along with an honest day's work and a clear mind, there were other refreshing developments. Social Services finally came to their wits and scheduled a final home visit. A formality, of course, but the ball was rolling. If everything went as planned, he'd have his daughter back. Chloe could come home.

2

Thursday, April 25, 2013

Tires screeched against the asphalt as Frank whipped the steering wheel, racing home. As he leveled the El Camino, he glanced at the dash's clock, consumed by punctuality. He couldn't be late. It wasn't an option. It could, in fact, ruin everything.

Shit, 3:48!

His last job of the day didn't go as planned, running an hour longer than expected. As he lifted the front end of a Tacoma, the owner came pouring through the house's screen door, brandishing a baseball bat and wearing the rage of a madman. These confrontations happened from time to time, and Frank could almost always defuse the threat.

While locked up, Frank packed on twenty pounds of solid, lean muscle. It wasn't by design, but when you have two options: lift and eat, the results develop. Along with the new mass, the sight of his shaved head, Dixxon flannel shirt, and imposing demeanor usually halted the reckless few and their frantic demands. If the imposing sight didn't quash the situation, Frank's wits and quippy tongue resolved the disputes.

Today was a little different, though. The owner of the Tacoma wouldn't back down. The man's intent was on full display, refusing to stop his tirade. He stood his ground in front of Frank's tow truck, not allowing the vehicle to move, adamant about his car's release. Threats flung from the man's heated lips, forcing Frank to adapt and enact Plan B.

Understanding the severity of the situation, Frank removed himself from the chaos, opting for the safety of the truck's cab. There, he reached out to his boss and later, the police, as difficult as that was. When the black-and-whites finally arrived, the officers detained the man, escorting him to the back seat of one of their cruisers. With the threat extinguished, Frank finished the job and only had a single smashed headlight from the encounter, but the distraction had other effects. He was running late and his Social Services caseworker scheduled the home visit for four p.m.

Squinting through the afternoon sun, Frank turned the old vehicle through the last turn of his commute. And to his delight, not a single black sedan lined either side of the road. He made it there first.

His rapid steps propelled him up the walkway, the anticipation building as he approached the door. With a trembling hand, he fumbled to unlock it and eagerly stepped inside.

Stillness invoked the living room's aura as he closed and re-locked the front door. Glancing around the space, he took in the silence. The drawn curtains filtered the afternoon light, casting a warm glow over the front room, but something felt off. His view shifted to the kitchen. The emptiness was stark, but the sight of the slightly open bedroom door on his right answered his questions.

"Mari? Hey, Mari, I'm home."

Reticence ensued.

Hmm. Maybe she didn't hear me.

Within seconds, he crossed the open room, aimed straight for the bedroom, but his momentum paused inches short. He thought he heard something from within as he approached, a faint set of whispers. Maybe it wasn't a set. Maybe more.

What the hell . . .

"Mari?" He leaned forward, ear turned toward the dark opening, wondering why she wasn't responding to his calls.

Nothing. Only the soft, rhythmic cycle of the floor fan's motor. No whispers. No other sounds reached his ears.

It had already been a long, stress-filled day, so he shook off the worry and buried the thoughts. As his fingers reached for the knob, the door swung away from him, opening up the bedroom for all to see.

Startled by the instant action, he pulled back, but the door's quick movement wasn't the only thing that flushed his nerves. Mari came barreling through the doorframe, nearly colliding with him. Her sight was downcast but readjusted once she realized he was in her way.

"Oh shit! Fuck, Frank. You scared me." With her heart racing, she reached up to her ears and removed the earbuds she wore. "Did you just get home?"

It took a few moments for Frank to collect his bearings, calming his fluttered pulse. He took in Mari, eyes hovering over her creamy skin and messy, wavy hair. He appreciated her more than she really knew.

"Sorry for sneaking up on you like that." He smiled, eyes narrowing in on the twinkle within hers. "Yeah, I just got here. Just came inside. I was calling you."

"Oh, sorry, man." She pointed to the iPod in her hand. "Tom Petty." She returned the smile and shrugged, soft wrinkles forming at her eyes' corners. "I was just checking on your dad."

"Oh yeah. How's he been today?" His view drifted to the dark bedroom, staring over Mari's slender shoulder. The lamp's dim glow highlighted the side of his father's bed.

Mari glanced back, taking in the room she'd just exited. "He's uh . . . he's been really quiet today. Just sleeping." She refaced Frank, but the warmth from before flooded away. "He didn't really eat either."

Frank bit the side of his cheek. "Yeah, I had trouble getting a few bites from him last night too." He paused, thinking about the pureed potatoes he'd prepared the evening before. "He's declining."

Mari delivered a slight nod, knowing the truth. "I know. And I'm sorry." She let the words settle before continuing. "Hey, why are you home so late? Isn't your appointment at four?

Like, right now?" A seriousness that seemed foreign replaced the easygoing nature she typically wore.

"It's a long story, but yeah, it is." His eyes widened. "Like, right now, Mari, and I need your help. Time is not on our side, but this place needs to be ready for them."

3

At 4:06, the sound of car doors shutting echoed from the street. Frank stopped his frantic bustle, attention fixed on the front door. Social Services had arrived, and they brought his daughter.

After ushering Mari out the back door, Frank stood guard in the center of the living room, anticipation brewing. His mind fluttered with worry, wondering how many boxes he'd left unchecked. Breaking his gaze from the door, he glanced around the apartment a final time, searching for mistakes or hazards, but the place actually looked tidy and organized. It still didn't flush the feelings lingering in his gut, though.

Voices just outside, amplified by the overhanging awning, and they were approaching. Frank attempted to count the distinct signatures: one, two, maybe three professionals. He wasn't sure.

A strong rapping came from the other side of the door. Frank's eyes widened, watching the door pulsate with each sudden strike. This was his moment, his time to prove to the world that the old Frank was buried six feet under. His palms grew clammy, and an icy shiver ran down his spine, but he couldn't reveal his nerves. He had worked too hard to fail now. It was go time.

Hurrying forward, he unlocked the dead bolts before gripping the doorknob. As he twisted it, a deep breath escaped his mouth, and he shook away the last fragments of fret.

I've got this. I've got this. Be cool.

With the pep talk fresh in his mind, he opened the front door. There in front of him were two adults. One was a stringy, aging male with salt and pepper hair, nearly his height, wearing black slacks and a buttoned white shirt. A name badge was clipped onto the right chest pocket.

To the man's right was a woman, probably in her early thirties. Frank had met her during a previous meeting, and he had already formed an opinion about Ms. Walker. Neatly clipped to the back of her head, her hair was a striking shade of black, adding to her overall polished appearance. She looked like her second home was a gym, and the smugness she carried made Frank's teeth clench.

Frank took little time considering the two professionals. His attention drew to the child standing between them. Young. Reserved. Chloe.

Looking up at Frank, her uncertainty and timidity were unmistakable in her eyes. She had only seen her father a handful of times in the past few years. She barely knew him any longer, but her memories hadn't tarnished. This was her daddy, the man who carried her, played with her, cherished her. The only person who bothered to teach her how to ride a bike, a skateboard, and patched her up when she fell and skinned her knee.

"Hi, baby." Frank's words were soft and deliberate. He leaned down, getting to eye level with her. "Welcome home."

4

Frank gazed at his daughter, staring into her light blue eyes. Eyes just like Claudia's. The eight-year-old returned the look, slowly shedding her reservations. She rested on his hip, feeling his strong arms wrapped around her waist and backside. Safety filled her mind, knowing the pain and loss were finally over. But she also thought about the trauma that still festered.

Ms. Walker and her counterpart, Mr. Jones, casually walked around the apartment, peering into cabinets and testing utilities. Their nonchalant conversations as they inspected the place fueled Frank's discord about the entire experience. He hated this, but he also knew this was the last test. After today, Chloe would be his again.

As she shut off the sink's tap in the kitchen, Ms. Walker called out to Frank, never directly looking his way. Her eyes were scanning the scuffed wall near the back door before taking in the square cat door cut into it. "Your paperwork states that you live alone. Is that correct, Mr. Collins?"

Frank cleared his throat, eyes darting to the woman. "You can call me Frank." He gently lowered Chloe to the floor as he forced a smile in the social worker's direction. "Um, no, actually. My father lives here too. He's elderly and needs my care."

"You'll need to update the forms." Ms. Walker stepped toward the refrigerator and opened it, kneeling down to inspect the contents, or the lack thereof. "Our system requires accurate documentation for all residents living in a household. But I'm sure you are aware of that, right, Mr. Collins?"

"Of course. I understand. That's not a problem." Frank looked down at his daughter and smiled, hands resting on her shoulders. "I'll fill them out and get them to the office tomorrow."

Ms. Walker shut the refrigerator door and continued. She ran her index finger along the counter's old tile before crossing the threshold into the living room. For the first time since she began the inspection, she registered Frank, making eye contact. "This apartment has only one bedroom, correct?"

Frank's view flew to the bedroom, but he also caught Mr. Jones exiting the bathroom down the same hall. "Yes. This is a one-bedroom apartment." His attention leaped back to the social worker.

"So the child will not have her own space. Is that correct, Mr. Collins?" The tone was more accusatorial than a genuine question.

"We're going to share the room." Frank could feel his heart rate escalating, and he didn't realize his grip on his daughter's shoulders had tightened. "I'm picking up a new mattress for her tomorrow. I have already paid for it."

Mr. Jones chimed in from near the bedroom door, "So the three of you will share a single room? In this quaint apartment. You, the child, and your *elderly* father?"

Frank's posture stiffened. He knew exactly where the two were leading. "It's hard to say this, but my . . ."—he paused, swallowing hard, before lowering his voice and praying Chloe wouldn't hear his next words—"my father's condition is dire.

He's in hospice care and will not be with us much longer. He's transitioning, I'm afraid."

The two social workers shared an emotionless glance, then hastened on, shoveling sand on the coals.

"You think it's wise to subject your daughter to this?" Mr. Jones asked, mirroring Frank's quiet tone. Surprisingly, his efforts were respectful to Frank and Chloe. "Emotional stress, such as losing a family member, can have a daunting effect on a child's mental health. Especially when this occurs in the household."

"I'm aware, but she has the right to say goodbye to her grandfather. I know it's been years, but at one time, she loved that man. And so do I."

"And your father." Ms. Walker continued, not masking her decibel level. "He's in there now."

Frank nodded, allowing the gesture to answer the question.

"We'll need to see the bedroom." Ms. Walker's stare shifted to the closed door. "Ensure the safety of the sleeping quarters—no exposed outlets, broken windows, you understand, right?"

"Yeah, yeah. I understand. Not a problem." Frank released his grip on his daughter and knelt, getting face-to-face with her. "Do you remember Papa, baby? Your grandfather?"

Chloe stared at her father, that wavering uncertainty returning. She remained still and mute.

"It's okay if you don't. It's been a really long time." He craned his neck, staring at the bedroom once more before returning his loving gaze. "But let's go see him. I'm sure he'll love being in your presence, baby girl."

Frank stood after Chloe delivered a weak nod. He held his stare, taking in her features: the innocence, the creamy skin like her mother's, the birthmark just under her jawline. Reaching out with an open palm, he wriggled his fingers, signaling for Chloe to take his hand, which she accepted.

"Right this way." Frank gestured toward the door with his free hand. With Chloe in tow, Frank approached the bedroom, followed closely by the two social workers. This was the last part of the inspection, the last hurdle in his sprint. He felt good about this and knew everything would right itself. In the coming days, he would have his daughter back.

5

A sliver of light penetrated the dark room, stretching out from the open door. Frank led the others inside the bedroom, feeling the warm touch of his daughter's hand in his. He didn't have to pull her along; she came willingly, and he could sense a hint of anxiousness from her closeness. But the feeling wasn't dread or worry, it was excitement.

As they reached the room's center, Frank's attention flipped to the two social workers flanking his right and left. His stare volleyed between them before calling out in a hushed tone, "Here it is. The bedroom, obviously. Not much to look at, but it's where we sleep." A subtle grin crossed his lips as he looked back at Chloe right behind him. "Where we all will sleep soon."

Ms. Walker had already stepped away from the group, eyes drifting toward the stained carpet and Frank's sagging twin mattress in the corner. Her counterpart stared ahead, fixed on the old man sleeping in the hospital bed positioned against the room's other wall. Neither commented for several seconds before she broke the silence.

"There's limited space in here. Where are you planning to put the new mattress, Mr. Collins?" This inquiry was direct, paired with a set of stern eyes.

Frank hesitated, trying to think, to stall a second or two. With everything happening in his life, he hadn't thought that far ahead. During the past few days, the only thing he thought about was having his baby girl back. It consumed his mind, leaving little opportunity for a thorough plan.

"Um . . ." He paused his response, trying to search for the words. He turned away from Ms. Walker, leaning down and making eye contact with his daughter.

"Can you stay right here, baby? I need to talk to the grown-ups for a second." Staring into her light blue eyes, he could see the caution swirling, the fear slowly taking a grip. It made him feel sick, knowing he was to blame, but he released her hand and stood. "Just a second, and then I'll be right back, okay?"

After calling the two over with a gesture, the three formed a tight triangle near Frank's mattress. Whispers followed, loud enough for Chloe to overhear but incomprehensible.

"I didn't want to say this in front of the kid,"—Frank paused, casting a side-glance at his daughter standing a few feet away—"but until my father passes, which could be any day now, maybe even before you release her to me, we'll sleep in the front room. There's plenty of space, and I think it'll be best for her well-being and mine."

Jones and Walker shared that similar, rejective glance before she contributed to the hushed conversation. "I'm still questioning whether this environment and what's coming is a haven for this child, Mr. Collins. Her *well-being*, as you say, is our top priority."

"As *I've* already said, miss . . ." Frank's voice grew sharp and cutting, his jaw clenched. He knew this wasn't the way, so he slowed his response, loosening the ratchet. "My daughter has a right to say goodbye to her grandfather. She doesn't have to be bedside when he takes his last breath."

Ms. Walker's hands rested on her hips. "Still, you need to understand our concerns here. This isn't exactly an orthodox situation you're presenting."

"Orthodox? This situation can't be that uncommon. Lots of kids live with a single parent and grandparents. This is *temporary*." Emphasis placed on the last word as he pleaded with his eyes.

"I know this means the world to you." Mr. Jones glanced at his counterpart, delivering a nod. "We both do, and we want to work with you, bring this dream to fruition." He paused his words, allowing a grin to replace the impassive mask he naturally wore. "Again, our only concern here is the child."

"And that's why you have to see this place for what it is." Frank's words were thoughtful, carefully orchestrated. "No foster home can give my baby what she needs. She needs me. She needs this."

The two stared at Frank, trying to peel away his facade's layers. Day in and day out, they worked with men and women just like him: impoverished, low-educated, living on government handouts, trying to scrape by on the cusp. They found no pity for him, though. They loathed the choices made and the pasts lived, disregarding the lack of an alternative. But they also believed in data and results.

The foster system was a gateway and a mess, struggling to provide adequate care for all the children in need. That was clear. Also evident was that a child in the care of their biological parent, free from any danger, was the optimal resolution to the issue. Frank's drug tests were clean. He had a stable, modest income and a roof over his head. Without responding, they both considered Frank's words, yet already knew their answer.

Ms. Walker extended her hand toward Frank, signaling an agreement. He stared down at it, heart hammering in his chest. He couldn't believe this. So many sleepless nights had passed, so many moments where he allowed the guilt and misery of Claudia's overdose to consume him. Was this real?

With his eyes beaming, he reached out and grasped her hand. Besides the handshake, all he could manage at the moment was to mouth the words "Thank You."

6

Frank and Chloe found themselves alone in the bedroom moments later. Ms. Walker abruptly cut off the whispered conversation and removed herself, opting to complete the paperwork from the well-lit front room. Dotting the i's and crossing the bureaucratic t's. Her partner, Mr. Jones, followed in her footsteps, leaving the bedroom door ajar.

"Hey." Frank's words aimed at the eight-year-old clinging to his right side now that they were alone. "Let's say hello to Grandpa, ' kay? He probably won't say much, but I know he's missed you. He even mumbled your name in his sleep last week."

Chloe's muteness continued. By choice or ability, Frank couldn't dictate, and he considered the newness of her setting. But he could see the shine in her eyes, even through the dimness. Those soft, wide, blue eyes painted the masterpiece he longed to create. She was safe, and more importantly, happy.

"Come on," Frank called out before turning his eyes away from his daughter. "He's right over here." He stepped in the hospital bed's direction, taking in the bundled-up old man. Before dangling his calloused fingers behind him, the warmth from Chloe's hand found its way into his palm. He paused at the feel, relishing the memories from a simpler time flooding his mind. All the work, the sacrifice. All of it had paid off. He had his baby girl back.

"Pops. Hey, Pops, someone's here to see you." Frank nudged Chloe around his side, feeling her frail frame slide past. His hands instinctively rested on her slim shoulders as they both looked forward.

With her repositioned to his front, he leaned down, stubbled face grazing her cheek. "It's okay. You can say hello. Even if he doesn't respond, he can hear you, baby. That's your grandpa."

Frank could feel his daughter's tension before she recoiled, but he held her firm. Sometimes the hardest tasks in life are those that you are guided through. And he would be her captain for this journey. He held an obligation to correct the mistakes of his past and manage her trauma.

"Go ahead, baby. Say hello."

Chloe glanced at her father, a brief side-eye before her gaze leaped forward again. After a few breaths, for the first time since she arrived, she spoke. A soft, single word, barely audible in the small room. "Hi."

The sound brought a smile to Frank's lips as he watched his father in slumber, the flaring nostrils, the soft snore coming from the cavern of the man's throat. Bittersweetness filled his heart, knowing he was losing his father yet gaining custody of his baby girl once again.

The two stood there for the next few minutes, cherishing the time, feeling their bond expand and multiply with each passing breath. Frank knew this was going to work.

His eyes drifted to Chloe, searching the girl, wondering if she shared the same feelings he was experiencing. As his view shifted back to his father, he realized something. Something he must have missed moments before. The old man hadn't moved, hadn't made a gesture or sound, but his face was different. There, painted on the man's lips, was a smile. One he was familiar with and had seen recently.

8

HOMECOMING

He crawled into bed hours before the new day, but sleep evaded him, teasing his consciousness before scurrying away. As he lay there hour after hour, staring at the ceiling, too many thoughts collided with his emotions. She was coming home. His daughter. Chloe.

After tossing the sheet aside, he swung his legs off the bed, bare feet mingling with the matted carpet. He sat on the mattress for a few moments, relishing the peace, the quiet, trying to suppress the anxiety fueling his sleeplessness. He knew it was too early to rise, well before the sun's rays crested the east, but anticipation loomed heavy.

The day lacked obligations, sans his daughter's homecoming. With careful planning, he reorganized his work schedule without any impact on his salary, while also leveraging the opportunity to gather potential favors from those willing to accommodate his changes. A simple sacrifice. Sometimes you have to give to get.

Rising from the bed, he tiptoed away and exited the bedroom in haste, leaving the door cracked. Despite having a packed agenda for the day, he couldn't ignore his father's needs that still required his attention.

The coffee maker whined in the kitchen, dripping droplets of energy and focus from its spout. He waited, watching the succulent black liquid slowly fill the decanter, savoring that first sip, that first taste. He hadn't always enjoyed the toasty beverage. No, the addiction he developed was different from previous ones, but he found it manageable and acceptable. One that Claudia shared during their years together.

Within a short span of time, he settled himself at the kitchen table, taking deep breaths to fully enjoy the enticing fragrances that surrounded him. A moment to himself, to reflect, to appreciate the wins. This was all he needed. The calm before the storm. But the familiar smells also awakened the past.

As the first caffeinated drops struck his lips, memories of his lost love slipped through the cracks. Claudia was always an early riser, and it didn't matter how hard they'd indulged the night before. The scent of a fresh pot always reminded him of the good times with her, and the agonizing ones too. The raging, belligerent fights.

Before he knew it, radiance beamed through the kitchen window, signaling the sun's wake from slumber. With the brilliant morning light, coos rang out from the neighboring doves and pigeons roosting in the palms. Today was the day.

Frank spent the next hours overanalyzing every detail, every blemish within this run-down apartment. He scoured the few dishes in the sink, toweling them off in frantic motion before putting them away. The bathroom was spotless, seat down, and for the first time since he could recall, had a pleasant smell emitting from it: lavender. A thoughtful gesture courtesy of Mari the night before. The vacuum also got reacquainted with every inch of the old carpet more than twice.

While wiping down the kitchen counter for the fourth time, a sudden pause in his heart occurred as he heard the melodious doorbell chime. That rigorous, circular scrubbing motion froze. Slowly, his neck turned, taking in the front door while his free hand rummaged in his pocket. He pulled out his cell phone. The clock registered 8:37.

It's too early, he thought. *Why are they already here? I'm not ready.*

Before he could settle his nerves, he crossed the open front room. He stood there, facing the door, fueled by a myriad of thoughts, memories, and feelings. His future was on the other side of this door. She was there, waiting.

But as he swung the door open, the anticipation crashed. There, standing in front of him, weren't some suits and his shy little girl. No. What his eyes revealed injected a new drug into his system. One he hadn't tasted in a while. It was Emma.

2

Two hours later, Ms. Walker and her partner concluded the visit. It was productive, and Frank shined like a newly minted nickel, leaping headfirst through every hoop. They noted his confidence and pride, knowing their decision was in all parties' best interests—especially the child's.

Despite the impression Frank painted, they still carefully planted advice and caution throughout the meeting. They referred to the positive words and phrases as constructive input, but he called bullshit on that; they were warnings. Just like the unannounced bimonthly check-ins that would occur, rain or shine. He was on a short leash, and one minor fuckup could derail the entire locomotive.

After walking them to the door, Frank regurgitated the last remnants of pleasantries and said goodbye. As he shut and locked the door, relief washed over him.

The forced smile grew genuine as he turned around, hearing a giggle in the room's center. In his cozy recliner, the eight-year-old girl happily spun in circles, thoroughly enjoying the sensation of being in motion. She looked at home, comfortable, like she belonged there. She returned the look, too, expressing a sense of hope and love. He stepped in her direction.

"Hi, baby girl." His sight hovered over the bleak area. "Excited to come home?"

A series of nods came from her while the revolutions continued, choosing not to answer vocally.

"I hope you like it here. I've worked hard, baby. Too hard to make this dream come true, but I'm so happy you're here."

The smiles and nods continued as she whirled round and round, unable to control the giggles. Amongst the light laughter, he thought he heard the word "dizzy" come from her lips. It melted his heart.

From the kitchen came the sound of running water. Emma stood near the sink, filling a plastic cup from the tap. Her brown shoulder bag sat parked on the counter. He'd barely spoken to her since she arrived, besides the initial awkward greeting.

Why did it feel so odd? he wondered.

As she entered the apartment, he tried to explain the imperativeness of the timing, but she insisted on caring for the old man, regardless. "Just a fly on the wall" was how she'd described herself. The red tape officials didn't object after meeting her, and with them in the distance, he felt they could share a candid conversation.

"Chloe. I'm going to talk to the nice lady in the kitchen, 'kay. Are you good?"

Through the playful fit, the young girl responded without glancing at her father. "Mm-hmm."

He stood there for a few moments, taking in the sights and sounds, a sense of accomplishment washing over him.

He met Emma just inside the kitchen threshold, not aware he was taking up the small opening between the two rooms. Ironically, the forest green scrubs she wore matched the plastic cup in her grasp. "Hi."

Locking on to him, she mirrored the greeting. "Hi back, just Frank."

He snickered at the playful barb. "Pretty crazy, huh?" He looked over his shoulder, taking in Chloe. Her escapades with the recliner had stopped, and she picked at a tuft on the chair's armrest. "I still can't believe she's here with me," he stated, facing Emma once more.

"It's incredible, but it's also a testament to your ambition. You wanted this, and you achieved it."

Frank could see the shine in her eye as she spoke, gleaming past the thick black frames. He took a moment to let the words sink in, allowing them to fill him with a sense of pride as he reflected on his efforts. "That's very kind of you, Emma. Thank you."

Her warm smile grew. "Indeed." She held her stare for a few seconds before glancing down at the cup in her hand. "Hey, this is for your father. He seems a bit dehydrated."

"Oh shit. Sorry." Stepping aside, he made way for her to pass through the opening. "Dehydrated, huh?"

Emma moved with a subtle shimmy, pausing under the threshold once they were face-to-face. The close proximity allowed the familiar scents of hand sanitizer and vanilla to tickle his nose.

"Yeah. I can see it in his skin."

Frank nodded. "It's been tough getting anything down him the past few days. The other nurses have said he's slowly transitioning."

Biting her bottom lip, her eyes shot downward for a split second. "He very well could be."

Frank stood in silence, giving her statement a chance to ferment.

Seeing the light in his eyes extinguish, she chimed in immediately, "But let me spend some more time with him. And if the diagnosis is what we think, just remember our role here."

As he nodded, she brushed past him, aimed for the bedroom.

Before she vanished into the darkness, he mustered the question he needed answered and called out to her, "Hey, Emma? Where did you go? I wondered if I would ever see you again."

She stopped in her tracks. After a breath and without looking back, she replied, "It's a long story, Frank, but one you deserve to hear. Give me a few minutes to tend to your father, and then we'll talk. I've discovered something that might alter our view on things."

With the statement fresh in his mind, he watched her disappear into the bedroom.

3

While waiting for Emma, Frank sat at the kitchen table watching Chloe doodle in her notebook next to him. A picture slowly morphed on the white page, depicting two people standing on a grassy hill holding hands. One tall, the other short. Fluffy white clouds adorned the page's top, along with a cleverly sketched sun wearing sunglasses. Both characters sported a smile that stretched from ear to ear, and lopsided butterflies danced around in the air.

He leaned over as she colored in the sun, then wrinkled his nose. "Hey, that supposed to be us, or somethin'?" He knew the answer, but a father never bypasses a chance at some sarcastic humor. Let alone a playful tease.

She cast a side-glance his way, dismissing the ruse with an eye roll.

"I'm just playin', baby." With caution, he reached around her back, placing a gentle hand on her shoulder and giving it a little squeeze. "Clearly that's Beavis and Butt-Head."

She brushed his hand away with a shrug, confusion sinking into her expression as she eyed him. "Who?"

An exasperated laugh leaked from his face. "Never mind, baby. Never mind. I know it's us, and it's beautiful."

A second playful eye roll came his way, but his attention quickly swayed from his daughter. Emma stood in the kitchen's entryway, eyes locked on the two sharing the intimate moment. She wore a smile, but underneath, there was an air of mystery. She gestured behind her, signaling she was ready to talk.

Chloe sensed the shift and followed her father's view. She stared at Emma, eyes full but holding caution. Frank had introduced the two earlier, explaining that Emma was a nurse who was there for her grandfather, there to help him.

Emma noticed the eight-year-old's glare and delivered a little wave, but no reciprocation came her way. The little girl dismissed the gesture without a sound and resumed her drawing.

Moments later, Frank excused himself from the kitchen table, leaving Chloe with a short list of ideas for her next masterpiece. He emphasized a beach scene (waves and sand and starfish), promising to take her on a vacation during the summer.

As he crossed the linoleum, he eyed the nurse standing in the living room with intrigue. Her abrupt departure the week before still stung, and he blamed himself, thinking he had pushed her away. But seeing her again, that smile, the warmth she radiated, pushed the worry and guilt to the side. He wondered what dish she was prepared to serve.

He met her near the old recliner, arms crossing his chest. "Hey, Emma. How's . . . how's my father doing?"

The warmth in her eyes dulled. She took a few moments to respond, carefully deliberating what to say. "I agree with the others, Frank. He is transitioning."

Frank stood there in silence, chewing on the words. He already knew the truth deep down, but he kept up the charade, telling himself otherwise.

"Hey,"—she reached out, gently massaging his bicep—"I know this is difficult to hear. But this is a part of the journey, and you served your role."

Tears welled in his eyes but never fell. He wiped them away with his palm, knowing they wouldn't do any good. He felt drained, empty. This day had already siphoned all the emotions he had left. "How long does he have?"

"That's not an answer for me, Frank. We don't make those decisions." Her eyes darted upward. "Only He knows for sure." She pointed an index finger toward the ceiling.

He felt a wave rush over him, one he hadn't felt before. "I know, I know." He released a deep breath, cheeks expanding. "What have you experienced with others in his state? Days, weeks?"

"Either. You just need to be here. He needs you now more than you'll ever know."

He let the words marinate, thinking about the past few weeks, the day he brought the old man home, the strange occurrences. After clearing his throat and wiping his eyes again, he thanked her.

The charm in her eyes inched back. "We'll do this together. We will."

Seconds later, an abrupt pause ensued. Frank could see a sudden transformation, a change in her posture. Her stance stiffened with rigidness. She still carried the inviting smile, but something else lingered.

"Anyway, I wanted to discuss something else with you, Frank. Something just as important."

He felt his muscles tighten in preparation. His mind teetered, wondering if this would feel like a walk in the park or a punch in the face. He leaned toward the latter, knowing his past.

"Yeah. Okay. That's good. I wanted to talk to you too."

"It's about the other day, right?"

"Yes. You just left one day and never came back. Why?" He knew he was the cause, but maybe hearing it would soften the blow. He also wondered why she returned. "What happened, Emma?"

"Well, ironically, that's actually what I wanted to talk to you about too."

"Oh." He felt the boil steady to a simmer, wary of the heat being turned up. "Okay, go ahead."

"Well,"—she paused her response and took a step forward—"you said something that day, something that rattled my cage a bit, Frank. Do you remember? The stuff about your brother morphing into the black creature."

He stared into her eyes, acknowledging what he feared from the beginning. This was his fault. Like everything else in his life, he had soiled this, defecated on something that could have been special. "I'm really sorry about that, Emma. I don't know what I was thinking. My mind was just . . ." His words trailed off as he dropped his stare to the carpet. "I don't know why I told you that."

"It was . . . disturbing." Breaths passed before she countered, throwing fresh kindling on the coals. "But the more I reflected on your dream, the deeper my brain delved into processing the information."

"And what . . . you think I'm crazy, huh?"

"No, no, no, no. Not that at all. You have your faults, like the rest of us, but crazy? No."

"Then what is it? What registered?"

Her eyes danced to the recliner for a split second. "Why don't you have a seat? This is going to sound like maybe I'm the crazy one."

4

Frank looked up from his recliner, watching Emma shuffle in place. She seemed nervous but also intent. His fingers gripped the armrests in anticipation, rubbing the peaks and valleys of the corduroy fabric. *What is it, Emma?*

"Frank," she began, hesitation loitering in her voice. "You told me in your dream that the dark figure spoke. Do you remember that? Do you remember what it said?"

Frank's eyes widened. Of course, he remembered. How could anyone forget something like that, something so vivid and personal? He dropped his chin twice, signaling his answer before following up with a verbal affirmation. "Like it was yesterday. That thing said—"

She interrupted him mid-sentence, "Your flesh shimmers like a sow's swollen teat."

The two locked eyes, feeling the tension slice like a knife. After a few breaths, Frank continued. "Yeah. That's exactly what *it* said." He cocked his head, searching her face and coming up empty. "Was that the reason why you disappeared? Why you left so suddenly that day?"

Her shuffling slowed with his words, transitioning into a gentle sway. But that wasn't the only change. The smile that had become a constant presence on her face suddenly disappeared, leaving him feeling unsettled. What Emma wore wasn't joy or hope. This looked like hopelessness or fear.

"That phrase, Frank. I've heard those words before, long before they came off your lips. I read them, actually. A long time ago."

His fingers stopped fidgeting with the recliner's fabric. "What . . . what are you talkin' about? How? What do you mean? When?" The fluster of queries fell from his mouth without a breath.

"Hold on. Let me explain." She held her hands out in front of her, palms open and slender fingers spread. "Just listen, okay."

Frank did just that, forcing his mind to slow. "Okay." He inhaled deeply through his nose, exhaled through his parted lips. With the pressure descending, he acknowledged her needs with a nod. "I'm listening."

With the bomb's fuse snuffed out, she continued. "When I was in college, I had to take some general education classes. Although my major was nursing, administration mandated that all students take prerequisite classes in specific fields." She paused, not only her speech but her subtle sway.

Frank nodded. "Go on."

"Well, one of those well-rounded courses was an art class." As she looked down at him in the chair, her black frames slid down the bridge of her nose. Using her index finger, she nudged them back up. "Historical art, actually."

Frank sat there, trying to connect the dots. "'Kay."

"Are you familiar with Hieronymus Bosch?" The look on Frank's face answered the question. "Anyway, he's a six-teenth-century Dutch painter. Some proclaim him as the first surrealist of the time."

Frank scratched the side of his face. "Emma, what is this about? Why are you schooling me about some old dead dude?"

"Because it's important, Frank. This might shed some light or even answer some questions. It might help you understand what I've been doing the past week too." A sternness ascended with each word as she spoke, one he hadn't witnessed before now.

"I understand. I'm sorry. Please go on."

"Throughout the semester, our class delved into a multitude of Bosch's works. One of his lesser-known pieces is a painting titled *Dulce Caro*."

Frank nodded, urging her to continue.

"Well, for almost twenty years, I've kept this painting etched vividly in my mind. But not just the painting or its name, Frank." A brief pause followed, and she forced a swallow. "The caption in the textbook written under the painting still makes my skin crawl."

Frank leaned forward, and he could feel his muscles tightening. "Why? What did it say?"

The room fell into an eerie silence, heavy with unspoken tension. Through the black glasses, Emma's narrowed eyes focused sharply on Frank's anxious face. The silence stretched on for heartbeats, unyielding, until Emma's voice abruptly shattered it.

"What did your brother say to you in your dream, Frank?"

Frustration surged as he responded to her question. "Emma, I already told you. Why are you . . ." Frank's voice trailed off, followed by the still, the quiet from moments before. His eyes dropped to the floor, and a rush of truth flooded his mind.

He looked back at her, face drained of color. "You can't be serious, Emma."

With her arms crossed tightly over her chest, she stood there, her head shaking. "Why do you think I reacted the way I did? It wasn't what that thing said, Frank. No. That phrase has hidden in my memory for decades, hibernating, and then out of nowhere, your voice awoke it from slumber."

"What? That's not possible."

As he spoke, Emma dropped her gaze and started toward the kitchen, leaving him speechless. He watched her sidle up to the kitchen counter, searching through her bag until she retrieved a hefty hardcover textbook.

With a single hand, she held the book up for him to see, the worn cover revealing its age. "Page two hundred thirty-seven, Frank."

Frank leafed through the book, his fingers tingling with anticipation as his eyes darted from one page to the next. There had to be a mistake, a misunderstanding. Or maybe a simple coincidence. A situation where Emma convinced herself of a deeper connection. He was sure the latter was true.

Page two hundred thirty-six.

As he turned the final page, there in front of him was a photograph of a painting. It lacked vibrant colors, but the imagery was vivid. Even without formal education or knowing its background, the painting's depiction was clear. From a gaping hole in the earth's crust emerged horrifying creatures straight out of nightmares. Monsters adorned with horns, bat-like wings, and cloven hooves ripped two females apart, flesh and blood strewn across the image.

Underneath the macabre scene was a phrase written first in Latin and then translated into English. *Caro coruscis sicut porca. The flesh shimmers like a sow's teat.*

Frank had to read it twice to fully comprehend what his eyes were witnessing. His gaze drifted from the page, landing on a waiting Emma. He sat there in silence, feeling the crushing weight of the truth before he forced the words from his lips. "This isn't possible. How can this be? That's exactly what that thing said to me in my dream."

Emma returned the stare, but her expression lacked the confusion dripping from his face. Confidence, absolutism smothered her features. "I know. And that's what I've been doing this past week. Research."

"You've been researching some old dead painter?"

"Yes. I think there is a connection here. Some historians claim Bosch was mad, a tormented lunatic. His memoirs suggest he possibly suffered from psychosis, but I also discovered something interesting."

"What?"

"Based on these memoirs, he had illicit, vivid dreams. Darkness clung to his psyche, filled with the things of nightmares."

"Why are you telling me this?"

"I'm telling you this because, over time, these dreams showed in his art. Demons and the things of depravity. Before too long, it was his only means of finding creativity, but it came at a price."

"Yeah, and?"

"Based on his letters, the illicit dreams also suggest that maybe something else was happening to him. Something unnatural. He claimed to hear whispers and see shadows while he painted. They haunted his thoughts, teased his mind, Frank." Beyond the black frames, her eyes narrowed. "Does this sound familiar?"

"Emma, this is crazy. It sounds like paranoia."

"Okay. But maybe this paranoia wasn't just what happened to him while his eyes were shut."

Frank remained silent, listening to her lecture, trying to force the abstract jigsaw pieces together. All he could muster was a shake of the head.

"What I'm trying to say is, I believe Bosch was a sick man, but I also believe that the illness came from something far more sinister than genetics or the slow deterioration of his mind."

"What does this have to do with me, Emma?"

"Listen, I have a theory. Picture this: when a mind shatters, evil can seep through the cracks. This phenomenon has the power to twist perception, manipulate its host like a puppet on strings. I think Bosch carried something with him, and his self-induced abuse allowed it to jump aboard. And . . ."

She paused, her tongue motionless, as she pondered what to say next. "Based on your dreams and what you told me about your father, I think something similar is occurring here.

He gawked her way, unsure of how to respond. Everything she threw at him was speculative and full of what-ifs.

"I know how this sounds, Frank, I do," she countered, seeing the conjecture swimming in his glare. "But there are too many coincidences here to ignore. I'm a woman of faith. Always have been, and I know there are evils out there in the world, ready to cripple and maim for His sake. I've seen them."

Frank's brow furrowed as he listened to her, confusion laced with pique. "His sake? Like the—"

"Don't say the name," she blurted, cutting him off. "Don't use it, don't think about it, Frank. We don't need to strike that match."

9

BEDSIDE

EMMA LEFT THE APARTMENT before lunchtime, leaving in haste. The constant hustle and bustle of a cycling field nurse. She had others to care for on her route. Frank understood and respected that, but to his surprise, she promised to stop by before her shift ended. There was a need in her eye, something new that Frank hadn't seen before as she said goodbye. He hoped she would come back. He needed her to come back. There was an overwhelming amount of questions that left a lingering discomfort. Her words rattled him.

With lunch on the horizon, his mind teetered away from the worry and confusion Emma planted in him. He'd come back to it, but for now, he had to bury the thoughts, as challenging as that would be. Chloe was home, and he had some fatherly duties to attend to.

His vision hovered inside an open drawer. Mismatched pieces of cutlery (spoons and forks and a single butcher knife) cluttered the surface, compliments of a neighborhood thrift store. A daily mental reminder of his finances. Each piece bore heavy use, the scars of time and tarnish. But what the drawer lacked in organization, it made up for with practicality.

"There it is," he mumbled. Clenched in his fist was a butter knife dulled with age. The right tool for the right job.

After unscrewing the jar's lid, he stared at the contents, savoring the creamy, smooth texture, the rich scent teasing his nose. Even though he practiced this dance regularly, it was almost nostalgic. With the expertise of a gourmet chef, he deftly slathered a slice from the loaf before combining it with a second already coated in a lavender spread. These days, peanut butter and jelly are a staple, an inexpensive avenue to nutrition. And he was grateful that Chloe shared the love.

His footfalls sounded heavy on the linoleum as he strode from the counter, carrying his daughter's sandwich and the one he made for himself, each wrapped in a paper towel: dual usage as a napkin and a plate. But everything seemed amplified now. More in tune, heightened.

Once he dropped Chloe's sandwich in front of her, he took a seat. He watched as the young girl engulfed the meal, taking bites large enough for a grown man. The scene brought forth a chuckle, but his mind drifted while he watched.

He couldn't shake the thoughts planted by Emma. The nurse's mention of shadows and whispers, the dead painter, seemed to spin in an endless cycle, like a never-ending loop. Everything she brought forth, the theories, the evidence, had to just be a simple coincidence.

This is crazy.

His eyes drew to his waiting sandwich, appreciating the neatness of his work, but his mind was still stressed.

Maybe she's the crazy one. Searching for something that's not there. A snipe hunt. There's gotta be a logical explanation. There's no connection and nothing is happening in this house.

Without another thought, he reached down and picked up the sandwich.

Minutes later, he dropped the paper towels into the garbage bin, noticing a difference in weight between the two. Through her best efforts, and as ravenous as her actions showed, Chloe failed to eat the sandwich's crust. She opted to conceal it within the crumbled paper. Frank smiled as he unraveled the loose folds, unveiling the square patterns of whole grain sweetness. He'd have to teach her the importance of finishing her meals, but pettiness wasn't a priority now.

With his daughter satisfied and hunger suppressed in his own gut, Frank's attention turned to the old man. Days had passed since a morsel of solid food slid down his father's throat, but the man still had a thirst. One that needed quenching regularly.

Besides the glass of water he poured, Frank warmed a can of chicken broth on the stove, testing it periodically with his finger. Before the temperature peaked, he turned off the burner, letting the broth simmer for a few moments. With the meal in hand, he approached the bedroom.

His advance stopped as he glanced at Chloe, now lying on the living room carpet, doodling once more in her notebook. Max had surprisingly joined her, watching the young girl create her masterpieces. She didn't acknowledge Frank as he stood there.

"Baby, I'll be in the bedroom. Taking care of your grandfather, okay?"

Her scribbling paused, and she looked up from the paper and smiled. "Okay," was all she replied before the frantic hand movements returned.

Shaking his head, Frank continued forward and disappeared into the dim.

2

Frank wiped the old man's chin. The task was arduous, but a few sips of broth found their way down his father's throat. Today, there was a noticeable difference. The result was comforting. He wanted to do more, but this was a win.

He left the bowl and glass of water sitting on the floor. He'd worry about them later. Right now he just needed to vent, empty the ill contents chafing his thoughts. His father couldn't reciprocate, but he knew his words wouldn't fall on deaf ears. The gasps and grunts told him all he needed to hear. Frank, Sr. was still in there, somewhere.

"Hey, Pops. I hope you can hear me." Frank sat in a folding chair next to the bed. His heavy shoulders sagged as he spoke, "I just need someone to talk to, okay?" The sickly scents of age hovered in the stuffy room.

Frank's weary eyes scanned his father, seeing the purple blemishes, the bruises on the old man's arm. "So much has happened, Pops. So much." He dropped his gaze, a slight shake to his head.

"That really nice nurse came back today. Emma's her name. The one that smells like vanilla." His head lifted, thinking about the nurse. "You met her last week. She's been taking care of you, changing your sheets, and trying to get you to eat." A brief pause followed as he thought about the many meals he poured down the drain. "She's been great, and she's coming back tonight to see you again."

The old man tensed, shifting his body a few inches on the mattress. Frank paused at the sight, eyes gleaming and leaning forward. "You can hear me, huh?"

As his rant continued, he sensed some life returning to his father. The old man's skin tone warmed; the gray hues slowly dissolved and presented a hint of natural complexion. His words seemed to have a positive impact.

Charisma returned to his voice seconds later. "Chloe's here too." A wan smile grew across his face. "She came to visit you earlier, remember? It's been a long time since you saw her. She's grown so much. She's so big. I can barely carry her."

The subtle shift in the old man's appearance invited him to continue shoveling away the layers of stress. A therapeutic remedy for himself as well.

"She's staying too. I have full custody, Pops. Those bureaucratic assholes can't say shit anymore, either. She's here for good, and she's not going *anywhere*."

For the first time in nearly a week, a sound not associated with a wince or grimace came from his father's lips. It was low and muffled, but it sounded like speech. Frank inched forward, leaving the sturdiness of the chair's steel seat. His hands gripped the bed's railing, and he turned his ear toward his father.

"What was that? I'm here, Pops. What did you say?"

Shallow breathing. The sound reverberated, engulfing the space. Inhale, exhale, but no words mingled amongst the breaths.

Frank's head rotated, coming within a few inches of his father's face. He held the pose, studying the old man. The prominent green veins hidden under the old man's temples were faint, barely noticeable now. "Did you say something?" he whispered. The old man's eyes fluttered beneath his closed lids.

"Yeah, you said something, and you can hear me." He fixated on his father, watching the rise and fall of the man's sunken chest. The constant motion was rhythmic, comforting. Almost hypnotic.

Seconds passed, but time seemed to still. Frank grew deaf to the room, hearing only the pounding of his own heart, not the fan blades in the corner nor the old man's breathing. A shift in the atmosphere followed. It suddenly felt warmer in the stuffy room.

Frank pulled away, a slow, deliberate motion. As he eased back into the chair, his eyes shifted around the room, feeling a disturbance. The steady penetration of shadows lining the walls lacked their still posture. From every direction, they grew, widening and painting the room in their wake. The lamp in the corner dimmed with the advancement, its light fading away like a dying ember, leaving the room engulfed in a somber darkness.

He sat there, immobile in the blackness; his limbs and tongue constricted by an unnatural force. A paralyzed prisoner in the unknown's grip. His efforts to eradicate the binds, to liberate himself from the constricting grasp, proved futile. Whatever was about to happen, he would bear witness.

Gusts of heat tinged his lobes, accompanied by something he couldn't fathom: uncanny whispers. The same he heard in his dreams. They echoed around the room, teasing from every angle. The faint, foreign voices penetrated his mind, seeping through his skull.

And then his eyes betrayed him, for what he was witnessing wasn't possible. All Frank could see was a dark silhouette's torso rising from a lying position. The shell of his father, this broken old man on his deathbed, sat up. The motion was slow, unexpected. Frank exerted all his willpower to recoil and break free, but his efforts were in vain.

The lamp's brilliance returned seconds later, yet it brought no comfort. No. All it did was confirm the impossible. There in front of him was his father, sitting up. And the man's wilted old head now faced him, eyes tightly shut.

3

Adrenaline released, fusing with the unimaginable fear coursing through Frank's veins. His breathing stopped, eyes glued on the face before him. But something had changed. His father's features, once defined by deep wrinkles carved into his jowls, now appeared less prominent, with only faint traces of sunspots peppering his forehead and scalp. Still elderly to the eye, but not a corpse waiting for the train ride.

The old man's eyes sprang open, causing a shudder through Frank's core. The whispers intensified with the act, hammering in his ears. He gasped at the sight, ending the few moments without a breath. But it wasn't the sudden, unexpected motion that rattled him. It was what lay beyond his father's barren, emotionless gaze.

Frank's father's eyes had rolled, exposing a glimpse into the depths of something unnatural, something unearthly. A crusty mixture of yellow and brown stared back at him, devouring his strangled nerves to get up and run away. But this wasn't the worst of it.

He could see the shadows surrounding him. Talons and claws emerged from wisps of blackness, materializing and striking at his flesh. The paralyzation slowly gave way, and he flinched at each attack, trying to block the violent swipes with his forearms and hands. Yet, the attacks left no wounds.

Suddenly, through the agony and trepidation, it all stopped. The shadows, the whispers, the phantom limbs, all of it. With his heart digging through his chest and beads of sweat dripping down his brow, Frank found himself in stillness. The nightmarish moment ended, but it wasn't over. His father still shared the space. The old man still sat upright in bed, head turned his way.

Frank broke through the terror and retreated from the bed. The folding chair he sat in collapsed to the floor as he backpedaled, unable to break his gaze from the scene. As he approached the jarred door, the old man's lips parted and a sound leaped from the blackened hole. A hiss, but also accompanied by a demand, "Bring me the girl."

10

THE OLD MAN

A SPLIT SECOND LATER, Frank threw the bedroom door open. It slammed against the wall with a resounding thud, and he rushed through the opening. He barreled into the living room, his momentum threatening to send him crashing into the recliner. As he righted himself, his eyes darted back to the black, lifeless doorway, expecting the pernicious shadows to give chase, to seep through and claim their bounty. Yet they didn't come. With each swing of the pendulum, torment filled the air, but the evils remained stagnant.

A timid voice sounded to his left, shattering the still. "Daddy? Daddy, what's wrong?" Frank whirled at the sound, his heart pounding like a jackhammer. His daughter sat at the kitchen table, a blue crayon clutched in her grip. Her eyes were wide, and Frank could see the uncertainty devouring her thoughts.

"*She's mine, Franky.*"

Frank froze, glossy eyes locked on his little girl. "Who said that?" The whisper crept off his tongue.

"*Bring her to me.*"

In a frenzy, he spun in circles, searching for the source. His stare volleyed high and low, taking in the four walls and ceiling.

This voice, deep and carnal, filled with spite, swirled around him. "*I need her, Franky.*"

The venomous demand morphed into a maddening chant, clawing and ripping its way through his cranium. It entered and exited his thoughts, striking him in a constant attack. "*Bring me the girl.*"

Without knowledge, he clasped his hands over his ears, teeth clenched like a vise. "No, no, no, no, no. This isn't real. This isn't happening. Get out of my head!"

The room spun, fueling a nauseating effect. Frank could feel his stomach churn, prepared to pop and release the madness. But as he slowed and steadied his feet, reality and focus came rushing back. His eyes landed on the eight-year-old in the kitchen. She stood now, backside hovering over the chair. Her mouth hung open. But the worry from moments before had vacated her face. She now carried something no father should ever see: unconditional terror.

"Chloe." Frank rushed forward, skidding to a stop on the linoleum. He reached out and pulled her toward him, fingers bracing the back of her head. She wrapped her thin arms around his waist. Her body trembled as it pressed against his embrace.

"Baby. Baby." He could hear a muffled sob as she buried her face in his abdomen. "Chloe, *shh, shh.* I'm sorry. Did I scare you?"

She glanced up at him and nodded, teary, hopeless eyes searching for answers. "What . . . what happened, Daddy? Why were you doing that?"

The look crushed him. He pulled her close once more. "I'm sorry. I'm sorry, baby. I . . . I don't know what—"

His voice died in his throat, and his gaping eyes shot beyond the lintel separating the two rooms. A familiar sound reached his ears, causing a shiver to run down his spine, one he prayed he'd never hear again. A serpentine-like hiss.

The deafening echo filled the air. Its infinite pulse sprang forward, invading Frank's mind like a burrowing parasite. And from her stiff, constricting posture, he knew Chloe could hear it too.

His eyes drifted down at his daughter. The young girl had craned her neck toward the source, and a tense shudder resonated throughout her body. The color drained from her already pale complexion, leaving her looking ghostly and ethereal.

Frank released his grip and moved to her front, shielding her from whatever evil lurked in the other room. He crouched down, bringing himself to eye level. "Chloe, listen to me. We need to leave. Get away from here, okay?"

Her lips trembled, trying to force the words to come. "What? What is that, Daddy? What's that sound?"

He ignored the barrage of questions. "Come on, Chloe." With a firm grip, he reached out and grasped her hand, pulling and guiding her past the kitchen table toward the back door. "We have to go. Now!" Spittle flung from his lips.

His stare drifted over the cracked, yellowing paint and scuffs in the wood—the kitty door he installed after moving in. With his shaky free hand, he twisted and disengaged the dead bolts. Each one unlocked with a distinguishable *click* that pierced through the infernal hiss behind them.

But then, his eyes betrayed him, revealing an unjust truth that wasn't possible. One by one, each lock reengaged, mocking the same sound that flushed his ears with hope seconds before.

"What the fuck is this?" Frank dropped his daughter's hand and fumbled at the locks again. With force, he twisted each open. Yet as soon as the last one's click rang out, all three locked back in place. "No, no, no, no!"

"Daddy! What's happening? You're scaring me!"

While he pounded the door's surface with the ball of his fists, the ominous sound reverberating from the bedroom ended. The sudden silence forced his hand, and he glanced backward. Nothing was there. As he tried the locks in a final asinine attempt, the nefarious command struck him again.

"Bring me the child, Franky."

The suddenness of the phantom voice ended his short-lived mania. Frank whirled around, weary, stricken eyes darting into the living room. He felt the icy grip of paralyzation creep over him, pulling him down into the depths. As his mind spiraled, sinking deeper and deeper, the front door rushed into his thoughts. But the idea quickly swept away like smoke in the breeze. If this unseen force can bar the back door, it can surely do the same to the front. It was hopeless to run.

Frank pulled Chloe into him, feeling her tremble, feeling the fear and the nescience on full display. She buried her face in his side, clenching and wrenching at his flannel shirt.

"What's happening? What's happening, Daddy?" Sobs quivered from her with each twist of the fabric.

He leaned against the back door, waiting for the inevitable, overtaken by helplessness. His eyes hazed over, smearing the scene with rot and misery. Darkness crept into his vision, blanketing the world in a veil of deception. And he felt the grim touch of unconsciousness carrying him away.

2

Memories strobed in his mind like a flash of lightning. They bloomed to life in a radiant burst, lingering just long enough for reflection: his childhood, his brother, Claudia, Chloe's birth. Each vivid episode brought him back to a time of happiness, a time when he didn't carry the weight of the world. Free from heartache and labels and the judgmental pain that persecuted his daily life. It was liberating.

Another flash ignited, blinding his sight. He held up his hand, shielding his eyes from the intense blaze. As it dulled to a calm warmth, the memories fused together, revealing something new, something different.

Frank glanced around this new setting, his eyes adjusting to an unexpected dimness. Walls confined him on each side, and heavy scents of smoke lingered in the air: stale tobacco and something else he remembered fondly. He was in a hallway.

There was a room at the end of the hall. Slivers of light outlined the doorframe, establishing a luminescent rectangle dangling in the distance. Instantly, he knew where he was. This wasn't a nostalgic memory filled with bliss like those that flashed before him seconds ago. No, he knew exactly what his mind was manifesting. This was Hector Martinez's house.

Without his will, he drifted forward in the door's direction. He never moved a muscle, yet he glided effortlessly, narrowing the gap until his advance halted right in front of the white door.

He knew what was hidden in this bathroom, what he would find if he opened the door. And he tried to turn away, hide from the truth that haunted his past, but he was powerless. Some unknown force held him firm in its grip, forcing him to live through this tragedy one last time.

He tensed as the door slowly creaked open, its hinges screaming for mercy. Inch by inch, more of the bathroom was revealed while a flood of light rushed his way. As the door continued its maddening arc, a figure came into view, sprawled out on the frigid floor. Feet, thin legs in black fishnets, a red minidress and matching Devil's tail. He had already lived this and knew it was her. It was Claudia. But . . .

Once the door's exhaustion ceased, reality capsized and descended into the darkness alongside Frank. It wasn't Claudia's lifeless face staring at him. It was a female, and she wore the same fogged, empty eyes. Congealed blood still streaked the nostrils and mouth. But this was the face of someone else. Under her chin was a blemish, an apple-shaped angel's kiss he knew too well.

"Chloe!"

Frank's screams pulsed through the hall, shuddering the walls. Fissures meandered along the drywall, leaving wakes of crumbling plaster falling to the ground. With each new crack that spiderwebbed through the rooms, intense light seeped in, devouring the vision in a glorified refulgence. And then it was over.

Taut pulls on his clothing broke him from the madness. He shook off the fog, rapid blinks refocusing his vision. As he stared down, he could see her face. His baby girl. Chloe. Tears streaked her blushed cheeks. She tugged on his flannel shirt, pleading for help. Despite her lips trembling and parting, her voice remained distorted and muddled.

"Chloe?"

Her words molded together, ending the hazy illusion. "Daddy! Daddy!"

"Chloe!"

The pain, the misery expressed in her eyes, her voice, tore his heart to shreds. For the past few years, he shared those same feelings, knowing his little daughter slept under another family's roof, knowing he was helpless to get her back and prove his worth, knowing Claudia was gone because of the poison he shoved in her face. Night after night, tears and sobs echoed in this apartment as he cried himself to sleep. But those days of self-torment and distress ended earlier this day. Chloe was finally home, and he would protect her with his life.

He peeled away from the back door. He searched the kitchen, looking for options, any means of escape. His view landed on the kitchen window overlooking the sink. But the thought died as soon as he saw the cold iron bars attached to the apartment's exterior.

The frantic search continued, fueling his unwavering need to free them from whatever was in his bedroom, whatever that thing was that posed as his father. He sure as hell wouldn't deliver Chloe to it or enter the living room where it possibly lurked, ready to pounce.

Then he saw it. His feverish scan landed and held. The small rectangular hole he cut into the wood days after adopting his cat. Max's door. The kitty door. It was small, less than a square foot, but Chloe's petite, thin frame was small too.

Dropping to his knees, he waved his daughter over, gesturing at the clear plastic flap filling the opening. "Here, Chloe. Here!"

She stared at the cat's door, barely able to speak. "I can't fit through that," she cried.

"You have to, baby. There's no other way. You'll fit. I know you will."

Reluctantly, she stepped forward and knelt, eyeing the ticket to freedom. "I can't, Daddy. I can't. It's too small."

"Chloe!" His voice firmed, not in an angry or punitive way, but with confidence, assurance. "Nothing's going to happen to you." His eyes glanced down at the door before returning just as quickly. "You will fit through that. Trust me, baby girl."

"But what about you?" She sized him up. "You can't fit through that shit!"

He ignored the swear. The moment was too intense to care about petty language. "Everything's going to be okay. I need you to listen to me." He placed both his palms on her damp cheeks, forcing her to calm the nerves racing through her veins. "I'll be fine. But I need you to go. Now, okay?"

She trembled at his touch, unable to answer.

"Okay!" Frank's confident voice returned, snapping Chloe out of the paralysis binding her in its hold.

With a meek nod, she lowered herself to the ground and penetrated the hole with an arm. The afternoon warmth smothered her skin from the outside. Another arm followed, and she contorted, squeezed her shoulders inward, making her as small as imaginable. With her limbs blanketing her face and head, she squirmed forward. It was tight, and the opening's crude edges scratched and tore at her flesh, but she fit. With a final push from Frank, she pulled herself completely through. While on his hands and knees, Frank watched as she regained her footing, peering through the opening.

"Bring me the child, Franky."

The plastic flap dropped from his tense fingers. Frank's eyes exploded, and he whipped around, taking in the sight behind him. A dimness spread throughout the living room, devouring the sun's rays in a ravenous feast. Like a shadowy serpent, it slithered along the walls, the floor, the large window, and the ceiling until an oppressive blackness consumed the room.

Frank dropped to the floor, lying on his side with his head near the cat door. He could hear Chloe's timorous shouts from the other side. He lifted the plastic flap, peering out into the beauty of the midday. White, fluffy clouds sprinkled across the blue sky.

"Baby. Baby, listen to me." He paused, catching his ragged breath. "You need to run, okay? Run across the way to the apartment in front of ours. There's a seven painted on the front door. A white seven. A nice lady lives there. Her name is Mari, and she'll take care of you until I get there."

"No, no, no. I can't." Chloe dropped to her knees, landing on the square slab of concrete right off the doorway. She reached for his extended arm protruding through the cat door's opening. "I don't want to leave you."

"It's okay, baby. I'll be there soon. I promise."

From the bedroom, the heinous hiss wreaked havoc once more. It moved through the air like a shockwave. Chloe screamed and released her grip on her father's hand, covering her ears from the venomous clamor.

"Go, baby. Go! Now!"

Chloe got to her feet in hysteria and sped off on wiry legs, vanishing beyond the apartment's corner.

Frank's glare shifted backward, seeing the onslaught coming his way. Tendrils of black mist sifted into the kitchen, clinging to the doorjamb with razor-sharp claws. They scurried along like a roach, engulfing the room with their stench. The walls, ceiling, and floor fell victim to their cancerous touch, left in a bubbling pit of decay.

Frank braced himself, his body frozen in place, as he witnessed the horrifying spectacle unfolding before him. The suffocating terror seemed to engulf him, ready to devour his very being. He could almost taste the imminent doom in the air, a bitter and metallic tang. In the deafening silence, his heart pounded in his chest, the rhythmic thumping echoing in his ears. With a surge of despair, he realized that this was the end, the final chapter of his existence. Yet, a small flicker of solace sparked within him, knowing that Chloe, at least, was now liberated from the web of betrayal. Before he could unleash the primal scream building within him, engulfing darkness descended, shrouding his world in an abyss of nothingness.

11

GUILT

"*FRANKY.*"

The whisper cut through the null, tugging at him.

"*Hey, Franky.*"

A nostalgic presence hid in the voice, lying beneath the surface. There was a comfort to it. The call rang out a second time, a little more audible, and it dragged him back.

He lifted his head, attempting to take in the world surrounding him. As he squinted, the vision slowly focused, blotches of color casting the darkness into the depths. A myriad of hues melded together before his eyes. He was calm, watching the setting morph together like a pupil observing an artist's strokes.

Yellowed grass, dying shrubs, a wooden fence stained a godly burgundy came into view. On his left, a grapefruit tree appeared. Its newly formed blossoms buzzed with life, sifting through the air and striking his nostrils. An outdoor setting clearly, but it was more intimate than that. He hadn't been in this yard since his childhood. He was back home.

"*Hey, Franky. Check this shit out.*"

The voice smothered him, locking him in an icy grip. It pulled out memories of his youth.

Mikey?

As he turned, a dark subject came into view, hazed and obstructed. An abstract portrait in defiance of its crystal clear surroundings. It beckoned him forward, waving a cloudy arm that bled into the air, leaving traces of peppered matter in its wake.

What the fuck is this? Am I dreaming?

"*Dude, come look.*" Its muddled face delivered a wink, distorting the view while it followed with another gesture. "*Hurry, Franky.*" Static attached itself to every syllable as it spoke, charging the air.

"Mikey? Is it really you?" The mumble oozed with disbelief, but the sight ushered in a warmth that he couldn't describe.

"*Get over here, dipshit.*" A sprightly chuckle drooled from its mouth. "*I have to show you something.*"

Without contracting a muscle, his body glided forward through the yard. His view drifted to the dead patches of grass below his sneakers before redirecting to the subject tempting him. With each foot covered, clarity claimed the scene. As the haze solidified, his belief came to fruition. It was his brother, only in his early teens, clad in his trademark black hoodie. The teen proudly displayed a shiner under his left eye.

Frank's advance stopped feet away, feeling the ground come up and take hold. With his footing established, his attention fixed on Mikey. His brother leaned forward, stare darting downward. Withered vines crocheted the ground near their feet, but something was there.

"What are we doing here, Mikey?" Frank asked, still questioning the vision's authenticity. "What are you looking at?" He mirrored his brother's look, leaning forward and trying to take in whatever lay mingled amongst the decaying leaves and vines. It was small and black.

"*Dude, do you see it?*" Mikey's voice expressed excitement, a trait Frank remembered vividly. The smallest flare of danger, of adventure or mischief, always sparked a side that usually led them to trouble.

The enthusiasm pushed into Frank as he listened to his brother's voice, watching the teen's thrill level percolate and boil over. This energy always steered him, regardless of the threat.

This happened. I remember.

Frank leaned in closer, hands on his knees, but the object's identity still lobbied in the unknown. "What the hell is it, Mikey?" he asked, never breaking his gaze on the thing.

"*I think it's a pipe. Like for weed or something. I found it here under the vines.*" Mikey glanced Frank's way before redirecting and pointing to where he had separated the entanglement of vegetation.

"Where did it come from?" Frank fixated on the object, kneeling and getting even closer. "Pops?"

"*Nah, that drunken bastard wouldn't touch the heavy stuff.*" Mikey joined his brother, kneeling over the object. "*He smokes two packs a day, but he'd never fuck with this shit.*"

Mikey reached down and grasped the pipe, holding it up to view. He rotated it in his fingers, taking in the brass fittings, the metal. "*Whoa, man. There's still some weed in the bowl.*" His glare bloomed with excitement, fixed on Franky. "*Should we—*"

I remember this. So long ago, but I remember this day. This was the first time that we . . .

"— *smoke it*?"

2

Shadows faded in, smothering the scene in misery. The darkness pulled at Frank, shrouding his thoughts and leaving the memory to rot. It was suffocating, the weight and pressure driving him down, down, down, forever falling into the depths, until . . .

Everything changed.

Light pulsed, vanquishing the constricting plague of black. The unbearable weight pulled away from his chest with it. As the scene manifested, he found himself in a car, the engine running. Rain fell from the night sky, pummeling the windshield.

I know this place. Why am I back here?

Slowly, he took in the car: dash, roof, windows, and *Mikey.*

His deceased brother sat next to him, his black hoodie pulled up, hiding his face. A scent crept off him, something pungent, spoiled.

Frank's glare fell to his brother's lap, seeing the man's fingers fidget in distress. They clenched and dug into the denim jeans he wore. The first stage of withdrawal. But he also noticed the strange hue of his brother's skin tone. A briny gray lingered there, festering amongst the green.

"Mikey?" he whispered, feeling an overwhelming surge of angst and threat carry into the car. "Are you okay?"

His brother sat there, unphased by the words, while the rain's orchestra beat down on the car, filling the silence.

Without another word, Mikey's neck pivoted, and he turned to face Frank. The streetlight above highlighted the man's face in a faint orange, but the scene brought out a gasp in the car.

Mikey's face matched that of his hands, a deathly gray coloring oozing with dark blotches of purple. The skin lacked elasticity, pulled tightly over his protruding cheekbones and eyes. But the worst part of the scene . . . the holes bored into his face and forehead. Three of them, each pulsing with the writhing movements of plump, white maggots. The larvae fell from the wounds, landing on his lap in clusters.

Frank found himself pinned against the door, shaken from the vision's torment. He watched as this thing, his brother's decaying corpse, opened its mouth and spoke. But it wasn't Mikey's voice. Something far more sinister leaked from the decaying skull's orifice. Something deep and carnal.

"*You murdered me, Franky. Dragging me here with false promises and self-indulgence. To this fuckin' alley. You knew what would happen here. You led me to my final resting place, a cold and unforgiving grave.*"

Frank couldn't counter. He was in shock, eyes wide and fixed on the scene. He watched as the shreds of skin moved and stretched tightly across his brother's jawbone, resembling snapping threads.

"I didn't know," he finally mumbled, never breaking eye contact. "I didn't know this would happen, Mikey. I swear, man."

But the guilt snuck in, regardless. For years, the event of that night haunted his thoughts, his memories. A daily reminder of his addictive past and the destruction it caused. The gluttony and hopelessness forced his hand that night, helping him steer the car into that dark alley. He was there for a simple fix, not the blood that replaced it.

"*My blood is on your hands, brother. There's no bringing me back, but you can still fix this.*" A fresh batch of maggots wiggled free from the bullet hole in Mikey's forehead. "*There's still time.*"

"How?" Tears welled in Frank's eyes as the words struck him. "How can I fix this? What do I have to do?"

"*You know what to do, Franky. It's the only way to shed your sin and shame. Do what is necessary, brother.*"

"But . . . I don't understand."

As the last word spilled from his mouth, a dense coat of darkness ushered its way in, blanketing every ounce of energy. In an instant, the rhythmic dance of rainfall fell silent, and the car and his brother disappeared. Frank could feel the load's denseness smother him, covering him with layer upon layer of uncertainty and hate. It piled on, pulling and tugging, tearing at his limbs, at his mind.

His heart thundered, ready to rupture from his chest as he gasped for a breath. But the exasperated gulps came away unquenched. Panic set in, followed by the only other thing his mind could convey: death.

3

The dark angel's frigid fingers never latched onto him. Instead, a radiant glow gleamed in the distance, barreling forward and extinguishing the coat of darkness. Frank had to lift a hand to his eyes, shielding himself from the encroaching brilliance.

The light penetrated his surroundings, circling him and filling the space. He suddenly felt embraced, like he was in the ethereal arms of safety. And then a sound spilled from the light. It was faint at first, an unknown distance from him, but as it looped, he recognized it as a voice. Closer. Closer.

"Who's there?" he called out, flushing away the illness from the previous dream. "Who's out there?"

An inky blot appeared in the center of the light, the rays bending and twisting around the form. It was a stark contrast with the glow, cloudy at first, but after a series of blinks, Frank could see that it was a silhouette. Someone was approaching, footfalls slow but close.

"*Franky.*" The voice drifted through the light on a stream of clouds. It was melodic, coursing with compassion, but the sound strangled him, and he felt his blood ice over.

No. This isn't real. You're not here.

The second call rushed his way as the figure slowly materialized. It was a woman. One he hadn't seen since childhood. Her blonde, wavy locks bounced with each step as she neared, sporting a smile he so needed in his life. The glow of her look rivaled the intense light surrounding them.

"*Oh, Franky,*" she cooed.

He stared at this goddess, overwhelmed by enamored emotions and sprinkles of resentment. She hadn't aged a day. A tear lay there, on the precipice of his eyelid, segregating his feelings and memories. "Mom? Is it really you?"

"*Of course, baby boy. I'm here. I've always been here, Franky.*"

Her soft words and warm glow infected his mind, a contagious pathogen spreading its tentacles and latching on for dear life.

"Wh-why are you here?" He felt his body gravitating forward, a moth to the flame. "You've been gone for so long."

"*I know, Franky. I know.*" Her eyes softened as she spoke. "*It's been a long time, son, and I'm sorry.*" Some reservation hid amongst the glow as he listened to her.

He held his tongue. The moment called for it, for silence. He just wanted to take her in, hug her, forgive her. This was his mother, Lynda Collins. But he had some reservations of his own.

For as long as he could remember, there had been a void in his life. And it drove him to self-medicate and seek the evils that could numb his mind and heart. He had forgotten how to love, how to cherish something. The afflicting emotion abandoned him years ago when he discovered she had left—moved away without a word, without an explanation, without saying goodbye.

He didn't know if he could ever love again. That is until Claudia burst into his world, followed a few years later by Chloe. With them in his life, the fire reignited once more, burning brighter than ever, regardless of his addictions. He shared that burden. And as he stood there, feeling the remorse and hope shed from her skin, he knew he had to forgive her.

"I'm sorry, too, Mom." Tears threatened to fall from his eyes as he reached out with both hands, cradling hers and intertwining their fingers. "I'm sorry you had to leave, about Pops, about everything."

"*Shhh, Franky.*" She stepped forward and released his hands, leaning into his chest while an arm draped his brawny shoulders. "*Everything's okay now, son. I'm here.*"

He mirrored her action, wrapping his arms around her. He held her firm, reveling in her touch, a mother's touch. The tears finally did fall, streaking his reddened face and splattering on the rotten ash below.

4

A period passed (a minute, ten, an hour), but Frank didn't care, nor did he break the embrace. He just continued to hold her and flush away the heartaches of a previous life. Now was a chance to bury the past and turn this chapter's page. He needed this to flush away the animosity and guilt. But like all moments of rectification and reprieve, it had to end.

Frank instigated the release once he felt complete. He stood there, a sway in his stance, fixed on his mother. He couldn't help but chuckle as he imagined how un-Frank he must appear at the moment. The tough guy, the loner, the man who doesn't need help from others, hugging his mother while a flood leaked from his face. It was all bullshit, a metaphorical wall to protect himself, but in this one instance, he let down his guard. He let her in. And he didn't even notice the wisps of black circling them.

As she watched him wipe the moisture from his eyes, she broke the lull that hung in the air. "*Oh, Franky. My son. How I've missed you all these years.*"

Her soft voice steered him. "I've missed you too. We needed you, you know? Me. Mikey. You left us without a word, left us to scrape by, to survive with Pops." A rigidness formed at the back end of his words.

"*I know, I know. That was wrong.*" She paused, biting her bottom lip. "*I ran from a problem and didn't consider either of you. That was selfish. I know that—*"

Frank didn't respond. Emotions pulled at him, each trying to steal the spotlight. He didn't know which would break through the barricade.

"*—but I swear to you, Franky, I'm through running. I'm here for good, here to support you, help you. I'm not going anywhere, s on.*"

A surge coursed through his veins as he absorbed the melodic cadence of her voice. Each word resonated with a reassuring melody, like a symphony of security enveloping him. The world, once blemished with uncertainty, now shimmered with promise. His mother was back, and she would never leave him again.

"Thank you. Thank you," was all he could muster.

She nodded, eyes sparkling his way. "*Everything's going to be okay, Franky. Trust me, son. Trust me.*"

He returned the nod, allowing all the animosity and confusion and abandonment to rinse away. Everything was going to be okay. The whispers assured it.

5

"*You trust me, right, Franky?*" Her blue eyes gleamed, piercing his soul. "*Right?*"

"Yeah," he replied, his voice laced with an undercurrent of anxiousness countering the need to please. "Of course, Mom."

She blew out a deep breath. "*I'm glad to hear that, son.*" Her voice filled with relief. "*Because I need you to do something for me.*"

He scratched the side of his face, brow furrowed. "What is it? What do you need?"

As she took him in, a change registered in her features. She dropped her stare to the ground and turned away, shaking her head. "*Never mind, Franky. It's nothing.*"

"No, tell me." He stepped forward, an overwhelming sensation steering him. "Whatever it is, Mom, I'll do it. I'll do anything for you."

She glanced his way for a split second before her eyes shot downward again. "*It's just . . .*" As she spoke, her soothing tone seemed to hang in the air, slowly fading away.

"What is it?" A smirk developed on his lips, seeing her vulnerability unfold. "You can ask me. It's okay."

She faced him once more, but the love and confidence she once carried were absent. A sternness filled with importance lived there, squatting in its place. Whatever was on her mind bore deep, leaving a cavity that ached with worry. "*Thank you. With the devoted support and undivided attention of their children, a mother's needs are guaranteed to be fully met.*"

"I'm here, Mom. I'm listening. What do you need?" he pleaded.

"*You do need to listen, Franky.*" She looked up and locked onto her son, burrowing her eyes into his mind while tension's blade sliced into the room. "*I need you to listen to him. Whatever he asks, you must do. Understand?*"

"What?" Frank's stare narrowed, the wrinkles in his forehead flexing with confusion. "What are you talking about? He? Who the hell is He?"

"*Oh, Franky.*" The phrase came out infused with pity and humility, followed by a sigh. "*You know who He is. You've always known. He's been with you for most of your life, and I need you* to grow up." Her voice changed with the last two words, charged with disappointment. The subtleness was instant, the flip of a switch. "*Do you understand, Franky?*"

Frank recoiled from the harsh glare, taking in his mother's anger, her chagrin. Even during his childhood, she had never chastised him or forced her authority over him. She was always the one who would listen, the one who would give advice, help him through his troubles. Who was this woman? His mind roamed, searching for an explanation for all this.

"*Are you deaf? Do I need to repeat myself, Franky?*" Her tone slowly morphed, a deep, guttural snarl attached to every other word. "*Do as He says, son. Whatever He says.*"

Frank could feel himself retreating, backpedaling. "I . . . I don't understand. What does He want me to do?"

"*Whatever is necessary,*" she hissed. "*Bring her to him, Franky. Deliver the child. You must.*"

He watched as his mother's bright blue eyes darkened, an unholy blackness consuming them, corrupting each with baneful intent.

"No. No. No. This isn't real. This is a dream. A nightmare."

He turned to run and escape the treachery unfolding before him, but a shroud of shadows blanketed the scene, smothering his will. Phantom whispers spiraled around, injecting their poisonous tongues into his psyche, and he could feel their razor-sharp claws piercing his sides, dragging him, pulling him into the depths. As he fell into the pit, a sense of emptiness overwhelmed him, and the darkness embraced him with its icy grip.

PART THREE

THE WRAITH

12

THE VESSEL

A WARM GLOW LOOMED in the distance. It began as a faint cinder, an orb of light, growing and devouring the surrounding darkness. Its ravenous appetite swelled, daubing the room's corner in brilliance and giving birth to shadows.

These ominous forms gnawed through the light's womb. They slithered and writhed along the walls and ceiling, filling the air with macabre laughs and stench. Obscure faces, teeth, claws, and the unthinkable forged in the blackness. They slowly encircled their prey lying on the floor, strands of acidic saliva dripping from their mouths agape.

Yet their insatiable thirst remained unquenched.

"*Franky.*" The stifled provocation sifted forward, easing into his consciousness. Audibly low and arcane, the voice pulled him from the void.

His right eye squinted open, fogged by haze and obscuring his surroundings. Worn, matted carpet kissed his cheek.

What happened? Where the fuck am I? Is this another dream?

As he lifted his head, the disorientation slowed to a crawl. He was in the bedroom. The lamp in the corner cast a dim light, spreading warmth across the way, and for a split second, it brought some comfort. He stared at it, blinking away the remaining fragments of confusion. But slowly, that contentness burned away. If he was in his bedroom, where was this thing residing within his father?

He struggled to his feet, feeling the wrath of vertigo. The dizzying effect nearly brought him to his knees. Reaching out for help, for stability, his fingers clenched around cold metal. As he righted himself, his view drifted to the object supporting his weight. It was a bar. The old man's gray blanket dangled lifelessly toward the ground from it. He stood in front of his father's hospital bed. The empty hospital bed.

A rush of panic pierced him like a syringe. His skin was clammy. With a sudden sense of foreboding, he froze, his eyes darting nervously from side to side, as if he could feel death's gaze upon him. Then he heard it. The deep, carnal voice that scathed and blistered.

"*Franky.*" The teasing tone sliced through the air behind him.

With angst, he turned and craned his neck toward the nightmare just feet away. Through his steadying vision, a dark silhouette lingered in the doorway.

Frank rotated around, taking in the creature and its stalking posture. His eyes grew wide as he took in the full presence of this monster. Its frail arms pivoted above its head, gripping the jamb, and its face hid beneath a shroud of darkness. An animalistic growl hovered in its labored breathing, and there was a subtle sway to its stance.

"*Where is she, Franky?*" Its tone changed, lacking any hints of playfulness now.

Chloe.

The memory pummeled him, and his mind leaped to the last moment he saw her. She ran off after slipping through the cat door.

Is she with Mari? Is she safe? Where's my daughter?

The shower of questions struck him one after another, and he could feel the anguish of uncertainty dragging him down. But he could also feel this thing's glare, eyeing him like a cut of prime meat.

He stared back at it, still not able to see its face. Somehow, he suppressed the fear raging through his core and lashed out, teeth clenched. "She's gone, and she's never coming back."

The thing's gentle sway suddenly stopped, and Frank could see a rigidness forming in its stance. An icy surge rushed through him as though a frozen river was flowing inside his body. For several tense seconds, it remained completely still before its head crept forward. As it penetrated through the shadow, the dim light revealed the true likeness of evil. His father's face stared back at him, but the hidden horror wasn't in the scowl or the lifelessness dwelling there. No. It was the man's eyes. Pitch black and void of human qualities. The eyes of the beast.

2

Frank jerked away, his lower back slamming against the hospital bed, but the impact went unnoticed. Never averting his stare, he recoiled further, rounding the bed and finding the room's wall. Trapped.

The thing took a single stride into the room, bringing an army of shadowy claws and fangs with it. They peeled off the room's surfaces, lunging Frank's way with mouths full of razors. He cowered, arms outstretched defensively. A bloodcurdling scream escaped his lips as the first set of teeth latched onto his forearm, ripping through his shirt and tearing his flesh.

"*Enough!*" The command slithered from the thing's lips in a long hiss, and its rabid battalion of shadows halted their attack, ending their encirclement and falling back from their wounded plaything. Snarls and giggles penetrated the room with their retreat.

The shock was overpowering. Frank couldn't feel the wound, and his ears rang with the speeding beat of his heart, but he could see the damage. Tendrils of crimson dripped down his arm as he inspected the bite. The teeth didn't penetrate deeply, but long slices of flesh gaped open. Valleys and rivers.

"*Where is she?*" Its deep, guttural voice sent vibrations through the space.

Frank's attention dropped from his bleeding arm and shot to the voice, taking in the monster standing before him. "Wh-wh-wh . . ." he stammered, not able to find the words.

The thing glared his way, dead, black eyes hovering over him, inspecting him, searching him. "*The girl, Franky! Where is she?*" The demand shook the room.

The suppressed pain finally shot through his arm, causing him to wince. He released a sharp breath as he clutched at the wound, bringing his arm tightly against his torso. "What . . . what is this shit? Who are you?"

The thing's focus moved past locating the girl, deception coiling around its tongue. "*Who do you see?*"

Frank took in the blank, emotionless stare returning his way. He shook his head in disbelief. "No. You're not my father. You can't be. Who are you?"

The entity posing as his father scoffed, clicking its tongue. "*You know who I am.*"

"No, you're not him. You're something else. Something inside him."

A millennium seemed to pass before the thing countered. It stood there, hunched over, its sunken chest heaving with each deep breath. "*I'm you, Franky. I'm your darkness, your passenger, your confidant.*"

Frank's body stiffened, cradling his maimed arm. Confusion and a smidge of agitation slowly replaced the shock and fear grounding him in place. "The fuck you talking about?"

"*When I found you in the shadows . . .*" The thing cocked its head left, vertebrae cracking in a satisfying sequence. The pops, each one different from the last, resonated through the room leaving its own unique mark, like a fingerprint. "*The bond fused easily. It was your vulnerability that first attracted me, the powerless intuition. Your lecherous appetite for indulgence. Your addiction. But with* her *death, the desire no longer burned.*"

Her? Claudia?

The thing's glare deepened, and a sly smile crossed its lips. Not one of joy or happiness, but an edacious smile. "*Yes,*" it hissed. "*Claudia.*"

Frank felt the hairs on his arms stand on end and saturation covered his pores. "Are you reading my mind?" he mumbled.

Whispers rattled around him, spiraling the room: distant, close, infernal. "*You killed her. You killed her.*" They closed in on him, penetrating his ears and skull. The taunts burrowed into his consciousness. "*Claudia. She's gone because of you. Her blood is on your hands. Claudia.*"

Frank squeezed his palms against his ears, ignoring the drops of blood sprinkling his shirt. "Stop it! Stop it." His eyes clamped shut and he gritted his teeth. "Get out of my head! Get out!" He felt the ground pulling at him.

Instantly, the maddening barbs ceased and a quiet tension lingered. Frank's shaky body slowed to stillness. His eyes sprang open, seeing the room's spin come to a halt. Slowly, his vision focused and landed back on the monster's blank glare. His weight drifted back, shouldering the wall in defeat. "What . . . what do you want?"

"*You already know that answer, Franky. You've always known. But first, let me excavate your buried memories.*" Without giving Frank a chance to respond, it continued. "*Years have passed since our bond was severed. The day you started your sentence.*" The thing glanced down at its frail, shrunken body, eyes hovering over the rib cage, the bedsores. "*This is my vessel now, my prison, but our days are growing short.*"

A drop of sweat meandered down Frank's brow. "Vessel? What?"

"*I've lain dormant, unable to break free from the shackles you bestowed upon me. And you bore me now. We've had our fun, but the blood of youth is near and I can taste it.*" It licked its dry, cracked lips. "*I need it, Franky. I need her.*"

Frank understood now. This creature didn't want Chloe to feed off her like it fed off him all those dark years. It *needed* her for survival.

"No, no, no, no, no." Frank pushed himself off the wall he leaned against, straightening up. "No, you can't have her. You can't have my baby girl."

"*Bring me the child, Franky.*" The thing paused, lifeless eyes taking in the ravenous shadows pulsing above it. "*Her savory scent is still fresh.*"

Entrapment consumed Frank's mind like a vise, its jaws crushing him, inch by inch. This thing, this parasitical demon devouring his father's last days, demanded the unthinkable. He couldn't lose Chloe again or deliver his only child to the belly of the beast. No. He had to think, come up with a formidable plan to get away, find his daughter (was she even with Mari?) and run. Just run and never stop, if that's what it took. But with the monster barricading the door and the security bars outside the window, there was no escape. But he wouldn't lose this battle without taking some swings.

"*Tsk, tsk, tsk.*" The creature clicked its tongue, eyes burrowing into the infinite depths of Frank's tainted soul. "*The clock is ticking, Franky. Choose.*"

As Frank returned the glare, a surge rushed in, coming from a place he didn't know existed. It carried his will, pushing him and pumping an infusion of strength into his body. "No." The word reeked of defiance.

The thing's labored breaths slowed, its once heaving torso now almost motionless. The lamp's glow from the corner highlighted in its dead, black eyes.

"She's gone." Frank readied himself, shoulders squared and fists clenched, prepared to fight, prepared to die protecting his little girl. "And I won't help you or let you go after her."

The thing's neck cocked to the right almost to a ninety-degree angle and its bony shoulders rolled, releasing a symphony of pops. A sneer crept across its lips, but there was more to the look than just contempt. Something else hid there below the surface.

"*The hard way it is.*"

As the last word dripped from its clenched teeth, a skull-piercing buzz rang out, devouring the empty static in the room. It amped up with each passing second. Frank dropped the tough-guy act, palms protecting his ears from the deafening clamor. But the sound also delivered a scene of primal chaos.

All around the room, the evanescent reins harnessing the shadowy beasts clinging to the ceiling and walls dissolved. Frenzied from their release, they lashed out at one another like a pack of starved hyenas. The frantic violence intensified, transforming into a swirling vortex of darkness where claws tore and teeth gnashed in a relentless storm. A pool of devouring madness tearing itself to shreds before forging together again.

But the turmoil and clash abruptly ended once the buzz faded away, leaving a lingering stillness wafting in the air. No sound, no motion, no command from their infernal master ushered its end. The raging beasts all paused in synchrony, a multitude that seemed endless. Each one's hollow, empty stare slowly turned in Frank's direction. Their glare penetrated, steadied on a new subject, a savory dish slathered in blood and flesh.

Frank's jaw dropped, seeing the posing threat evolve. The entire ceiling oozed and writhed with the inky silhouettes of distorted creatures reared on their haunches and ready to spring. He stood there helpless, knowing he was about to be torn to shreds.

3

The swarm came seconds later, engulfing Frank in a sea of ink. The strikes were implacable: mauling, scratching, clawing, gripping his flesh. They pinned him against the wall, stringing him up, thrashing his body and mind until his kicks and screams ceased.

As the dawn of silence arrived, the sweeping cloak of shadows slowly peeled away, revealing their battered and bloodied masterpiece—the newest addition to their gallery. Frank remained affixed to the wall, bound by wisps of darkness chafing his wrists and ankles. His head hung, chin dangling against his chest. The swift beating had left him lifeless.

Suspended there, his breaths came in ragged gasps, barely registering in his own consciousness. The pain was stifling, and he longed for the agony to climax, but the suffering and torment were far from ending.

Through his blurry, swollen vision, a faint movement drew his attention. A dark, elongated, apparitional tentacle glided through the air toward him. It cupped his chin with delicate precision, lifting his head before sliding around his throat.

As the mist-like thing constricted, Frank's eyes popped open, feeling the oxygen leaving his shambled core. There in front of him was his father's passenger, his leer void of human qualities.

Frank struggled, sinewy muscles contracting in his arms and shoulders, pulling and wrenching, trying desperately to break free. But the binds were unforgiving, and his struggle to suck in air was failing. As his eyes welled and darkness sprinkled his thoughts, the monster continued its exigency.

"*Where is the child, Franky?*"

With his jaw clenched, he shook his head. No matter the agony this thing inflicted upon him, he remained resolute and refused to yield.

"*So be it.*"

The tightness ratcheted, and a veil of gloom covered his sight. With it came the strangling thought of suffocation. It carved its way into him, shoveling away the dissipating courage that was about to kill him. He couldn't give up his baby girl, the only reason for his depressing existence. Deliver her on a plate and spoon-feed this demon. But what other option did he have? If he died here and now, the thing would just send its army of darkness into the world and drag her back. And he would never know her true fate.

"Okay, okay!" Frank cried, barely able to form the words. "I'll do it. Just stop this! Stop, please!" His welled eyes finally breached and a single tear rolled down his cheek.

As the last word escaped his lips, his father's host body waved a rail-thin arm in the air, and the strangler released its grip. The appendage slithered away, melding with the other forms in the black pit.

Frank gasped and choked, feeling the life-giving air assault his lungs. As he slowly recovered, sucking in deep breaths, he felt the shadowy restraints binding his wrists and ankles loosen. He fell to the floor below, face-first, collapsing like a sack of potatoes. His fingers writhed through the matted, stained carpet, trying to clutch the strength to lift his woozy head. And he finally did. But the view only continued the turmoil.

Stepping to the side, the thing created a clear path out of the bedroom and gestured at the opening. The view showed the living room, the recliner, but also the sights that stretched out beyond it. The front door hung wide open, and for the first time, Frank realized the hour. In the night sky, the moon cast a radiant glow, illuminating everything around. Across the common space and the walkways, he could also see Mari's quiet, dark apartment.

4

The next few minutes were excruciating. Frank shuffled out of the apartment, hunched over, cradling his battered ribs. His fingertips gently stroked the bruised tissue. He winced at the touch. Misery coursed through his body with each laborious stride. Broken. Shattered. The pain in his core, his sides, arms, and legs nearly brought him to his knees, but another pain forced him onward. Chloe.

The idea of dragging her back was sickening, and it crushed his soul. How could he agree to this? How? This was his child, his blood. Her lone existence pushed him away from ending it, from pulling the trigger. And now . . .

Fuckin' coward.

As he crossed over the sidewalk segregating the properties, echoes, snarls, and yelps sounded behind him, coming from the cavity of his blackened apartment. It sounded like a crazed feeding frenzy, ramping up with each passing heartbeat. The chaotic explosion erupted into the cool night, and he found himself frozen.

His thoughts drifted, thinking about the waiting beasts' salivating jaws and ravenous hunger. The claws and fists that had already destroyed his body. Chloe wouldn't become their next victim. No. The demon needed her, but what would become of her? Would it slowly corrupt her, steer her toward death? Pump her full of the shit that still haunted his nightmares? Would she be another victim, like his beloved Claudia?

He couldn't do it, wouldn't do it. As agonizing as the torture was (and would be as soon as he returned), coupled with the intense dread of suffocation, his crying pleas were now empty. A facade to buy an ounce of time. A chance to break free and deliver a final warning to his baby girl before the lights snuffed out for eternity. He could die a content man if she knew the truth and if she was safe.

His legs felt heavier as he continued his romp, forcing the muscles to obey. He waded through the murky depths, feeling the siphoning ground suck and pull at his feet. Yet the effort paid off. There in front of him was the door. Mari's door. Apartment number seven.

He shook from panic, from the unforgiving pain racing through him, yet somehow he drew the strength to reach out and grip the cold brass knob. Was she even here? Hiding inside, burrowing her face in Mari's side? Was she frightened, an emotional, hysterical wreck? Wondering where her deadbeat father was? He gave it a twist. Locked.

He leaned to the right, the pain firing in all his nerves. His muscles contracted, spasms running the length of his taut frame. He seethed through the agony, jaw clenched as he searched for life inside. The large window that mirrored his own was dark, curtains drawn. Not a sliver of light pierced the perimeter. Either they *were* hiding, or they had fled.

He leaned against the door, sweaty forehead resting on the surface. He had to soothe his aches, slow his racing heart and ragged breaths. But he also had to find them, get their attention before it was too late.

With grit, he mustered some strength and pushed past the affliction. He pounded the door's surface with the ball of his fist. Slow, steady strikes. "Mari! Chloe! Open the door! Please!" The pleading words started with conviction but slowly morphed into a brittle cry and sobs. "Please, please!"

There was no response, no answer. No affirmation of his daughter.

With dejection, he gave up, body turning sideways and sliding down the door's surface. He sat there and wept, clutching his heart and mumbling his daughter's name. He moved his head to survey the hellish entrance of his home. The monstrous calls poured from the blackness, wailing his way. They called for him, luring him back into an infinite purgatory.

He sat there for an eternity, listening to them, banging the back of his head against the door, screaming for the agony to end, for the pain to soften and vanish. As he did, a horrifying abomination unfolded before his eyes. One by one, the shadows crawled out through his open front door, fangs and talons bared, glistening in the moonlight. They swarmed, engulfing the night on their way to claim their bounty.

In an instant, the horde was on him, and a squelching blackness snuffed out the grains of hope. Before it consumed him, his mind fired a final synapse: a memory of her, Chloe.

13

THE BLOOD OF YOUTH

FRANK FELL TO THE floor once they dragged him back inside. Hard. The impact was unforgiving, spasms shooting through his core like a freight train. He lay there, grimacing, a broken toy. The constant flow of pain etching its way through his body was the only reminder that he was still alive, still breathing. But he could taste death's sweet nectar. He could feel the darkness calling for him. It wouldn't be long now. There's only so much a body and mind can take.

His eyes fluttered, trying to grasp the scene and focus. Slowly, his eyes presented a macabre scene. He was back in the apartment, surrounded by the afflicting horrors. The shadows oozed from every surface, morphing and melding together, a diabolic concoction shaken and stirred. And their master was still there, too, ready to drop the guillotine.

This imposter, this virus seeping within his father, hung close, its menacing eyes drilling into the shattered remains sprawled out on the floor.

"*Where is she?*" The scorn layered in each word stung like a hornet.

Frank didn't know where Chloe was. She must have fled with Mari, and hopefully, they were long gone. It was the only explanation. Otherwise, one of them would have heard his pleas and opened the door.

He lifted his head, turning toward the vengeful proclamation. He held the look, unable to do anything else, while the taste of copper rinsed the back of his throat.

"*Then you leave me no choice.*" The thing's glare lifted, taking in the voracious pack waiting in the wings. One shadow separated itself from the horde, its abstract cranium nuzzling into its master's hand with affection.

Frank rolled onto his side, wincing from the shifting pressure. Through his clenched jaws, he muttered a single asinine word, "Please." His bloodshot eyes mirrored the sound.

The thing returned its glare, holding it for several seconds in silence before breaking the lull. "*You bore me, Franky,*"—it paused, letting the words cut like a machete—"*and you no longer offer relevance. I'll find her myself.*" Its eyes drifted up again, prepared to send the beasts out into the cool, dark night.

Frank struggled through the damning truth, but the message shone like the moon in the heavens. This thing didn't need him. He was a pawn. An insignificant piece dangled and led to the chopping block, like a lamb to slaughter. Those creatures would scour the city, aroused by his daughter's youthful scent. They would hunt her down just like they did him, until they dragged her back here. Back to Hell. Unless he could stall. Give them enough time?

Straining with every ounce of grit left in him, Frank pushed himself onto his hands and knees. "No, wait."

The thing's face flexed as if considering. Slowly, its view landed back on Frank, watching the shattered man get to a knee.

"Please, wait. Stop. I know where she is." Frank sucked in a breath, feeling the knives slice through his lungs. "Don't send them. I can do it."

It had grown tired of the games, patience no longer a virtue. With a single swipe of its fingers, Frank's body elevated and crashed into the recliner. He tumbled to the floor, a discarded plaything. A thin laceration opened on his forehead, and the red life from within clouded his vision.

He lay there in a pit of misery, praying for the reaper's icy grip to end it, but he wouldn't be so fortunate. Once more, an invisible force slammed into him, lifting him off the ground and crashing him against the wall. It held firm, stretching his limbs outward like a five-pointed star, a new decorative fixture.

With each swift stride, the thing drew closer until it stopped, standing directly in front of its captive, face-to-face. It eyed Frank, staring at the contusions, the bruises, the blood dripping from his wrinkled brow. An artist admiring the latest addition to the collection.

It leaned in, a long sniff started at Frank's shoulder and ended at his ear. As the motion ended, it pulled back, revealing its ravenous appetite.

"*I will have her, Franky. You can't stall forever. I know what you are doing. And it won't work.*"

Frank tried to turn away from its blazing black eyes, but it was useless. Its glare penetrated his mind, scrambling his thoughts, while an unseen, deathly grip smothered his throat, holding his head in place. He couldn't hide his intentions, but what other choice did he have? Maybe there was one.

"Just . . . take . . . me." The cracked words spilled from Frank's mouth between gasps for air.

It clicked its tongue, eyes honing in, enjoyment resonating from its pores.

"I'm here." The veins in Frank's temple throbbed while he gasped for fresh oxygen.

The thing studied him like a lab rat, knowing the ploy wasn't over yet. "*No, we've had our fun, Frankyyyy.*" The last syllable elongated into a heinous hiss. "*I covet a new menu now. One that I sample again and again and again until her bones wither away.*" It glanced down at its body before redirecting. "*The wick burns low within this shell, demanding the necessity of a new carapace, a new host.*"

"Why?" The pressure on his neck intensified, and he could sense the darkness swooping in. "You . . . don't . . . need . . . her. Take . . . me."

The thing leaned in closer, their noses nearly touching, but Frank could feel the tightness ease up and his breaths came. An overwhelming feeling invaded his body as he stared into this creature's menacing, lifeless eyes. There was depth there, like an infinite black hole pulling him inside. He felt like he was floating, slowly consumed by the darkness.

"*You still don't understand, Franky.*" It snarled, a hint of annoyance lingering.

"Understand . . . what? I'm right here. Enter me."

The thing drifted back, breaking the intimate proximity. It flexed its jaw as it eyed Frank like a fresh cut of meat. "*The bond between us is dead without your abuse, and it will not fuse again, u nless—"*

The air felt stagnant, empty, as Frank waited for the beast to finish.

"*—the blood of youth is injected into your veins.*"

"What?" Frank's mouth hung open and droplets of blood dripped from his brow. "Youth?"

"*The girl, Franky. The blood. Her lifeline is a necessity.*"

The words escaped Frank's tongue, leaving the room soiled in silence, but his mind raced, trying to decipher this monster's riddles.

Blood? Chloe's blood?

"*Yes,*" it interjected in an insidious moan, satisfaction oozing from the word. A proud tutor cajoling its struggling pupil.

"*Her blood,*" the whisper gnawed through his ears and ricocheted through his skull, burrowing deep into his cranium.

"Get the fuck out of my head!" Frank spat, eyes clenched like a vise. His neck craned to the side, trying to recoil from the hideous leer. "No, no, no, no, no!"

"*The blood of youth is pure, untainted, and easily molded.*" This thing, this demon, moved its jaw an inch to the left, controlling the imperceptible strings anchored within Frank.

Against his will and buckling under the strained effort, Frank's neck turned, taut muscles threatened to rupture through the skin. He refaced the fraudulent patriarch standing before him, feeling its glare sear his flesh. Through the agony, his saturated, glassy eyes reopened, taking in the vile stare of death. Defeat singed the remaining threads of hope, and all he could do was plead, knowing it was asinine.

"Please. Not my baby girl. There has to be another way," he mumbled, quivering. "Please."

"*The ember has died, Franky. And your chance at redemption has ended with it.*" The demon strode backward a step, staring at the rearing beasts hanging from the ceiling. Their rapturous cackles and howls devoured the room.

"No." His weary head shook from side to side. "No, don't kill her. Don't kill my baby."

The demon's attention piqued, and it dropped its sensuous gaze from the calamity of evil clinging above. With loathing and indignation, its response squirmed from the black orifice of its mouth. "*If I'm to claim you once more, I don't need to bleed her dry, Franky. She is just an appetizer to enter your being. The innocent blood will open the door, and I have only to escape this bastille. Are you going to tell me where she is, or are you already a s useless as I presume?*"

2

Frank's heart thundered in his chest, and his ears pounded in rhythm with the raging beats. He didn't know where Chloe was, but he would not indulge this monster with his negligence. With all his effort, he cleared his mind, cementing his thoughts in an infinitely rising wall. As the mortar slathered the bricks, a solemn lull hovered about, burying his soul in a bleak pot of gall. He couldn't let this leech back inside his head.

His father's possessor held him in contempt. "*Your silence proclaims the answer. I'll find her myself and feast*"—the last word purred from his lips before he continued—"*upon her suc-*

culent flesh, Franky. I can still smell her, and her skin shimmers like a sow's teat."

Frank's eyes widened, his pupils contracting into focus.

The phrase launched a wrecking ball, bulldozing the cognitive barrier he built. It crumbled like a sandcastle after the rising tide. Instantly, his dejected eyes sprang to life, revealing strength he no longer knew existed, and a memory came crashing into his thoughts.

Emma.

"*Ah.*" It paused, a blackened, forked tongue licking its lips. "*The nurse. The one with the barrier surrounding her soul. Thank you for reminding me of her. What a prize she would be. So ripe and full of light. I would take my time with her, savoring every divine morsel, but her aura is too pure.*"

The words carried something Frank had not witnessed until now: disappointment and envy.

"*Much different from the other woman you delivered to me. Your fellow* junkie." Its face twisted into an impish snicker, and Frank knew exactly who he referenced.

"*That is the term used to describe your kind, is it not? Junkie, or addict? Degenerate? She is just like you, swallowing handfuls of pills to push the cravings away, to bury the pain. Oh, she was easy, Franky. A yin to the nurse's yang, as they say in this world. What is it, that salivating term of endearment you use for her again? M ari, right?*"

The name slipping through its treacherous lips struck him like a rod of lightning, and he felt his stomach lurch. Nausea hit him in a relentless loop. A rush of saliva filled his mouth, and he desperately gulped to suppress the insatiable craving, but it was futile. He popped, spilling his gut's contents onto his ripped flannel shirt. Another layer of despair mixed with the pooling blood from his forehead.

Frank could feel the warm embrace of unconsciousness swooping in. As his neck crumpled, his chin dropped to his chest, lingering there momentarily, until the demon's grip constricted around his throat, keeping his head fixed in position. Spittle strung from his bottom lip, lengthening until it snapped and fell to the floor below.

"*Not yet, Franky. We are just getting started.*"

Frank's saturated, glassy view hovered on the beast before him, feeling its fingernails digging into his flesh.

"*You delivered her straight to me, Franky. All it took was a simple touch to forge the bond, much like the shell I wear now. Much like you so many years ago.*"

"Touch?" Frank's jaws clenched in fury.

"*You don't remember, do you? The day in the courthouse. The day of your sentencing. Is it not so obvious?*"

"What are you fuckin' saying?" Frank muttered.

"*After the arrest, you had no access to fulfill your cravings any longer, and my control slowly faded. I had to feed, had to consume to sustain myself. That's where your father came in. Your father's deteriorating mind was an easy target. You put me here, Franky.*"

"No." Franky shook his head from side to side, breaking through the ironlike grip. "No. I didn't do this."

"*Yes. Yes, you did, Franky. It was the handshake, remember? The last one until your release. That moment when your rage peaked, and you lashed out at him. What phrase did you use again during that embrace?"*

Frank chose defiance, keeping his gritted teeth clenched. That memory was fresh, still cut like a knife, and it plagued his mind with despair. He hated himself for this.

"It was, 'This is the last time we will ever speak. You're dead to me, motherfucker. And I hope you die alone like the miserable, pathetic piece of shit that you are.' Your poetry, Franky."

The demon let the phrase loiter between Frank's ears for a heartbeat, stripping away any dignity the man had regained. The sight was enjoyable, and its lust and greed for more steered him forward.

"His mind was an easy opening to manipulate, to deceive and destroy the remaining purity. Easy prey, much like the woman across the way."

A long silence set in as they fixed on one another, enveloping the room in ambivalence. All of this was Frank's fault. He understood that now. He allowed this menace to enter his life, to enter his father, his apartment, and now it had infected the few he loved. How much influence did it have over Mari?

The image of the scythe's swift stroke consumed Frank's thoughts. He yearned for it. When would this end?

"But enough with the monologue, Franky. You don't deserve my words or my time." Its fingers released his throat, and it stepped back.

Fresh air filled Frank's lungs, his breathing coming in deep heaves. Exasperation and coughs filled the room as he recovered.

"*Either tell me where she is, or your life ends now. You can see her one last time and say your goodbyes. Forge the fuse with her blood. Or not. Either way, I will find her, Franky.*" The shadows' cackles and raucous howls peaked once more, blistering the air into chaos. "*And I will drive her into the ground.*"

This was it. His chance to embrace the end. To accept the inevitable. The darkness he craved, coveted. His pain, his suffering, the guilt, the self-loathing could all go away with one snap of his finger. And with it all the pressure and stress, the weight of the world would sift away like ash in the wind. He could finally find peace. But something held him back. He couldn't let this happen.

"Okay." The word dribbled from Frank's mouth. "Okay. I'll tell you where she is."

The demon considered him, searching his mind. "*The last time we played this game, you failed me, Franky. You came away with nothing. My pets had to pull you back.*" Its eyes narrowed, excavating layers of Frank's consciousness.

"I know, I know." Frank swallowed hard, fixated on his target, the taste of iron thick on his tongue. "She wasn't there earlier. She never was. I tried to fool you. Throw you off. That won't happen again."

Silence smothered the demon as it scoured Frank with its black orbs. It chiseled away, skillfully brushing cognitive rocks and boulders to the side and unearthing the treasures within his mind. "*You're hiding something, Franky. I can taste it.*"

"No. I can't hide anything from you." Tears welled in Frank's eyes. "I'll get her back here as long as you don't hurt her. I'll take some of her blood so we can rejoin. That's the deal, right?" He paused, hoping to see some reciprocal understanding but came away empty. This wasn't a game he could win.

That was the deal, right?

Silence.

Through the moroseness, Frank's negotiating continued. "Let me go, and I'll bring her back. I promise. I just want to see her one last time."

"*Then tell me, Franky,*"—the demon's eyes narrowed, still scooping away sand and silt— "*where is she? No more games.*"

Frank's eyes quivered before he answered, "I . . . I told her to run down the street and, uh, hide. She's probably blocks away by now, but . . . but my voice will pull her from the shadows. She'll know it's safe if she sees me, hears me calling her." A series of nods followed the acquiescent guarantees. "Let's end this. Together."

The room suddenly stilled. Even the writhing infernal pool above came to an abrupt stop; their monstrous clamor snuffed out like a candle's flame. Frank took in the inky sea, watching the waves steady to a calm. His view drifted down, watching the beast detest him for several breaths, waiting and praying.

"*Together,*" the demon purred. "*Together again. Just like the old days, right, Franky?*"

"Yeah. Me and you. I'll do whatever you want. The drugs, the booze, anything. I'm ready. Just like before. Together."

"*Oh, Franky. Intrigue floods my loins just thinking about it. The savory serums coursing through your veins, your inhibition deteriorating before my very presence. Your*"—it wavered for a brief second—"*lubricious misery.*"

"Yes." That was all Frank could muster, along with a plausible nod. "Yes."

The demon's posture stiffened, a rigidness swallowing the rapturous hunger displayed. "*But how can our bond fuse if you can't find her?*"

Frank's brow wrinkled. "I can find her. She's down the street. She's hiding. I know she is."

"*No, Franky. She's not.*" A sway manifested in its stance. "*You're learning to hide your thoughts, but it's useless.*"

"I swear to you. I'll go and find her, bring her back. I will." Each word slathered in conviction.

"*Franky, Franky, Franky.*" Its tongue clicked. "*Enough with the deception and lies. Those skills fall under my umbrella of expertise, remember? You don't know where she is.*"

Frank's breaths slowed, and his heart dropped into his gut. "What the fuck are you talking about? She's down the . . ."

Slyness crept across its lips. Seconds later, it reapproached, leaning into Frank and whispering into his ear, "*I already have her, Franky. I just needed to taste your groveling and lap up your last drops of hope. A piquant cocktail to soothe my eternal thirst.*"

Frank side-eyed the beast hovering near his cheek, eyes blooming. "No, no, no. You don't have her. You don't know where she is." He tugged on the ethereal shackles, trying to break free from the binds. "She ran away. Miles away by now. She's gone."

The demon pulled back, a gluttonous grin consuming its wretched face. "*Your friend, Mari, has her, Franky. Or should I say, my friend?*"

"That's not true. You lie." Spasms twisted in Frank's body. He shook with violence, pulling and flailing his limbs. "No, no, no, no. You lie."

"Then who's at the front door, Franky?"

Shock set in, stifling the atmosphere. Frank's sight drifted from the demon standing before him, staring past it to the living room's entrance. The front door was closed—a tightly secured lid on this malignant sarcophagus—and seemed to pulsate with anticipation, contracting and expanding along with his breaths.

And then the doorbell rang.

14

INVITED GUESTS

A SECOND CHIME SHOOK his ears moments later, fueling the dreadful climb to the summit. Were they really on the other side of the door? Mari and his baby girl? Denial and dubiety raced through Frank, but the truth sank its fangs into him, and it felt like a sudden plunge off the edge of a precipice. This wasn't some vengeful ploy to torment him. It was real.

Veracity declared its legitimacy seconds later. One by one, the dead bolts disengaged with thunderous clicks, setting the stage for a climactic finale. As the door crept open, its hinges groaning with pleasure, affirmation burned like the scorching sun. They were there, standing on the slab of concrete, the moonlight dancing within their jaded stares.

The sight alone drove nails into Frank's casket, but the true murder weapon was the embrace they shared. His best friend, the only person he truly trusted, and his daughter stood under the rusty awning, hand in hand. It looked so natural, so amiable, like a mother and child on a leisurely stroll. Love denouncing the world's evils.

But the scene was a ruse, masked in a perpetual guise. Both were mere puppets in this act, strung along by the same ethereal cords binding Frank to the wall.

"*You see, Franky. She's been in my possession all along.*" The demon snickered, revealing some human qualities hidden until now. "*But watching you break, devouring your delectable pain, lapping up your secretions, that was blissful.*"

The matted carpet smoldered under each step as the demon walked in their direction, leaving a blackened trail of ash in its wake. Its advance stopped feet away from Mari and Chloe, holding both in its sights. Extending its arm toward the center of the room, it gracefully stepped to the side, inviting the guests to enter with a subtle gesture. "*Welcome.*"

Smiles blanketed their faces, but the lack of pleasure was evident. Manipulation, indoctrination? With the greeting, both stepped together in unison, a ewe and its lamb entering the cavernous gloom. As they neared the room's center, strides matching, the door's gaping mouth creaked shut, resealing the tomb. Frank found himself caught in the crosshairs of both their gazes.

With his bludgeoned, weary eyes, Frank studied his daughter's face, seeing the unnatural essence. Chloe stood before him, but something else had invaded her: a parasitical entity thriving for ascendancy. And its talons were already deeply entrenched.

"Chloe!" Frank thrashed, leaning forward, the diaphanous binds digging into his wrists. The tendons in his arms and neck jutted out, visible through his skin. "Baby, can you hear me? Chloe!"

Dismissing the outrage, the demon came up behind the two, clapping its slender fingers on their shoulders. Its glare mirrored those of the two visitors, zeroed in on the cut of beef pinned to the wall.

"*Franky, Franky, Franky. Your efforts are gallant but all the while cretinous. She's mine now, just like your beloved Mari, who has always been mine.*"

Frank ignored its sinful banter, his gaze glued on his daughter. "Chloe, I know you can hear me, baby. Just listen to my words. Everything's going to be okay. I promise."

"*Tsk, tsk, tsk.*" Disappointment dripped from each scoff. "*Oh, Franky. When will you ever learn? Your words are fruitless. And our time has concluded, leaving behind a bittersweet nostalgia that dances like sunlight on a tranquil sea. Rebirth is on the horizon, and my chariot to the gates stands before you.*" Its neck craned, taking in the smiling young girl on its left before leaning in and orchestrating a sensual whiff along the side of her face. "*Ooh, how I relish her flavor, Franky. A gluttonous confection I can taste until her heart expires.*"

"No." Frank's head shook with detestation. "No, that wasn't the deal. You are supposed to take me. Enter me again. Remember?"

Its cold, dead eyes left the eight-year-old, landing back on Frank. "*You bore me,*" the demon stated, contempt sprinkled on every word. "*And your susceptibility confounds me beyond wonder. Did you really believe that I would return to the prison and its decrepit walls?*"

"We had a deal!" Frank frothed. "Her blood and my body!"

"*And the great deceptor's wrath has struck again, son. If He's taught me anything, it's how to influence results in my favor.*" It paused for a tense moment, too long of a moment, before continuing. "*The game's over, Franky. Checkmate. And now, you will watch me ascend the steps to my new kingdom.*"

Frank's mind spiraled, weaving unfathomable webs of betrayal, hate, and melancholy. It was suffocating. Once more, he found himself a victim, duped by this beast. The air was heavy with the scent of deceit. His heart sank, burdened by the weight of humiliation, while the taste of treachery lingered on his tongue.

With Frank succumbing to the guile and defeat that ravaged his being, the demon's attention turned to Mari. It leisurely rounded her frame, then released its grip on her shoulder until all three of them aligned in a linear formation. All facing Frank.

The neighbor's face radiated with delight, her gaze unwavering as she followed its graceful and mesmerizing dance, her smile begging and pleading for sanction. The demon mimicked her stare, a mask of admiration cutting through the daunting canyons of wrinkles.

As the two shared the look, it whispered a phrase her way, "*Thank you, Mari. Thank you for bringing me the girl.*"

Though silence stole her tongue, her eyes sparkled like a shooting star streaking across the night sky, revealing an exuberant rebuttal.

"*Frank sends his gratitude as well, my love.*" The demon's gaze shifted, capturing the grief that dropped from Frank like the remnants of a dying rose's petals. "*Now, my dear, you can rest easy knowing you've completed your tasks. And you've fulfilled them with sterling diligence.*"

With the words freshly cutting through the air, Mari's neck pivoted, her view shifting back to Frank. Through the haze, he could see her. She held the look, the smile, the carefree qualities he adored and loved about her. This was his best friend, and he corrupted her by delivering this evil right to her doorstep.

"*But now,*" —the demon interjected, completing his lurid speech—"*as you no longer add value or relevance, I dismiss you from your duties, Mari.*"

Frank blinked away the saturation impeding his vision: the sweat, the blood, the tears. His eyes volleyed between the two while a feeling of rot brewed deep in his gut.

No, no, no. What does that mean?

With a simple flick of its wrist, Mari's neck snapped. The crack reverberated like a cannon, engulfing the room in its thunder. She stood there for what seemed an eternity, her cheek resting on the top of her shoulder. But eventually, her limp body collapsed to the floor, dropping like a stone. The sudden act severed the bond she held with the eight-year-old; their fingers no longer interlocked.

Screams poured from Frank, and he rattled his binds, pulling and tugging, every muscle ready to rupture. The rage boiled and spilled all over the room as the sight before him seared itself onto his retinas. Mari lay there, facing him, still wearing that warm, inviting grin. But the worst part was her stare. Her vacant, lifeless eyes locked onto him, piercing straight into his soul.

2

Sobs followed the outburst. The sounds grimmer than the percolating frenzy from moments before. Frank hung there, tears and snot dripping from his battered face. There wasn't a way to express the illness seeping through him, and he couldn't fight any longer. It was over.

"*Now that your tantrum has shed its skin, perhaps your new birth will allow us to continue,*" the demon mocked, a wispy eyebrow arched.

Frank lifted his head, barely able to hold it up to glare the beast's way. "You . . . you killed her." Frank's words fluttered from his lips, almost inaudible.

"*A strategic move, but one necessary to gain the advantage in this little game of ours. A bishop for a queen. Nothing more, Franky. She served her purpose well.*"

"Fuckin' murderer!" A sudden influx of hate steered his words and actions.

The demon's grin vanished, and a rigid expression burned deep in its posture. "*That is one label for my work, I suppose. Manipulator, corruptor, instigator being others. As you know from experience, I specialize in the slow deterioration of one's soul until my host can no longer heave a breath. So yes, I suppose the m urderer agnomen fits me like a glove.*"

"You didn't have to kill her! You could have just let her go! She did what you asked."

"*Where would the fun be in that, Franky?*" the demon scoffed. "*Besides, loose ends can have detrimental effects down the road. She was expendable, much as you are. And your wick is about to burn out, my old friend.*"

"But you need me," Frank insisted, voice crackling. "You can't do this without me."

The demon considered Frank's words, holding him in its sights. "*No, it's not you I need, mortal. Your shell is corroded, a deteriorating cocoon I no longer salivate for. The only thing I need f rom you is your blood.*" It paused, letting the words cut deep. "*A few drops will suffice. Just enough to change the anatomy of your dearest child here.*" A fond look stole Chloe's innocent face. "*An addict's impregnable genes.*"

"I won't do it." Detestation and defiance brooded in every syllable.

"*Oh, Franky. That's where you're wrong.*" It strolled behind Chloe, never removing its treacherous gleam. "*You'll do any- thing I ask. You always have been easy to shape and mold.*"

"That was before." Frank spat a bloody wad of phlegm at the demon's feet. "Now I know what you are. And your days of controlling me are over, demon! I won't do it!"

Its eyes narrowed, two piercing black stones slicing through their prey. "*Oh, you'll do it, Franky. You'll do as I bid. You always have and you always will.*" Slowly, its slender, withered fingers slid up Chloe's spine, cupping her nape. "*Your lifeline will course through her veins, even if it means sacrificing you in the process.*"

Frank found some grit, arching his back and holding his head with pride. "No!" he bellowed at the beast before him. "I won't!"

As Frank screamed the last word, the demon pounced, its body soaring through the air with an otherworldly grace. Land- ing upon its shattered target, its talon-like nails gripped Frank's throat. And then it squeezed. With the act, the vociferous clam- or from above erupted in hysteria.

Its face smothered Frank's, their noses smashed together. "*You. Will. Finish. This*!"

Its breath reeked of sulfur, suffocating Frank as it screamed and tightened its grip, draining the life from him. "*You will deliver your essence to the girl, Franky*!" Blackened spittle flung from its mangled jaws, speckling Frank's chin and cheeks. "*Do it or I'll drain you myself*!"

Darkness seeped in from all around, swallowing the light in gluttonous gulps. Frank's eyes felt heavy, buckling under the tremendous weight. He could feel it dragging him down, pulling him into its loving embrace. But it lacked comfort and pulled away just as quickly as it manifested. He wasn't ready and his role had yet to conclude.

With his lungs screaming and every nerve in his body begging for the pain to end, he muttered a single word, "Okay."

3

Frank crashed to the floor moments after waving the white flag, the binds withering away. His bones reverberated from the fall, and he lay there, insufferable pain shooting through his limbs, his core. Defeat settled in, dejection barring its nasty teeth and chomping down on him. Slowly, his sight came to, focusing on the carnage before him: Mari's body directly to his front.

The poor woman mirrored him: frothy, lifeless eyes staring directly at him, searching his soul. The spark had escaped them the moment her spine snapped, but the sight brought more than just morbid chills. It ushered the past to the front of the line. A memory Frank had revisited often, one which chiseled away at the remains of his heart.

As he lay there, falling into the infinite abyss of black, flashes of light barreled into him, contrasting hues of emptiness followed by brilliance. The strobes intensified in a rapid session, swallowing his vision until they stopped in a final translucent explosion.

His breaths were heavy, and a series of blinks fluttered his eyelids. With those actions, colors and shapes materialized as the blinding haze crawled to a halt, creating an eerie and unsettling scene. The vision before him had changed, an alternative perception of the truth. It wasn't his living room he glared at. And it wasn't the wrathful remains of his best friend sprawled on the floor. It was a dingy bathroom and on the floor was Claudia.

Martinez's place. Halloween night. The night the shadows finally drove a stake through his chest. The night they pushed too far, exposing themselves and ruining his life. The night *It* was victorious.

"*Get up. Now.*"

The sudden command shot through his mind, and he shook away the memory. It faded like fog dissipating on a sunny afternoon. There in front of him once more was his neighbor, his best friend, her neck grotesquely twisted.

"*It's time, Franky.*"

Frank's glare wavered around the room, finally landing on his father's possessor. The root of his misery and anguish. The demon.

Lifting his weary frame, he watched the smirk curl this monster's lips, its mocking leer skinning him alive. A child's magnifying glass above an anthill.

Frank staggered to his feet, fixated on the menace's haunting ambiance. Scorching heat rushed through him, every nerve and receptor singed by the fire. But he pressed on, barely able to collect his footing and face his future.

"*Your blood will spill,*" the demon stated, standing next to Chloe, holding him in contempt. "*And I will be reborn.*"

"How?" Frank's tongue felt like a strip of sandpaper, congealment loitering in the back of his throat. He could hardly form the words, but he forced them out. "How do we do it?"

The demon's eyes softened, tasting victory in the air. "*You will pour your life into her, Franky. Fill her with the disease that hinders your life. The savory infliction and plague that seeps from your pores. The act will erode her soul, and a fissure will form. An easy passage to enter her valley and take root.*"

Frank's face grew grim, drained of color. He couldn't fathom what he was about to do, but he understood he had no other choice. This was the only way Chloe could survive another day. Her life would be over, but at least her breaths would still rise and fall. And an overwhelming sensation took control.

The demon continued. "*Retrieve the blade from the kitchen. Bring it forth and fulfill your role.*"

Without a word, Frank shuffled forward, a marionette on strings.

15

FAITH'S RETURN

THE STEEL SHONE UNDER the fluorescent bulbs above, reflecting Frank's battered face. He held the blade at an angle, analyzing his injuries while also contemplating the severity and violence this tool could inflict. Was about to inflict.

Tears welled in his eyes as he closed the utility drawer and pivoted, prepared to do the unthinkable—to end his life to damn his daughter's. As he took a step toward the living room, his nerves reanimated, and a quaking shake pulsed through his body. A frigid reminder of his beating heart. He nearly dropped the blade in his wake but held firm, steadying his wobble.

With his free hand, he wiped away the saturation obstructing his sight and stepped forward, stopping under the lintel separating the two rooms. He reached out with the same hand, gripping the jamb for support, while the knife dangled near his thigh. From here, he studied the area, the tipped-over recliner, the beast and its stalking eyes, and the unfortunate view of his baby girl. She had swiveled in place, facing her patriarch and protector. The one man who was supposed to guard her with his life, blanket and shelter her from the world's evils.

Her stare was genuine. She still embraced the loving smile she'd walked into the room with earlier, hand in hand with Mari, and that toothy beam was directed right at her father. It crushed him more than this demon or its army of shadows ever could.

"*It will be . . . painless,*" the demon commented, breaking Frank's gaze from his daughter. "*And swift. A little pressure on your wrist and this will all be over.*"

Frank took in the beast, noting the hollowness of its eyes. The void of humanity. The depth where there should be none. Without a response, he nodded, his eyes filled with wetness once more. This was it.

He released his shaky grip on the jamb and shambled forward. His eyes volleyed between his daughter's loving grin and the calamity of black squirming and nipping from the ceiling. With another step, the beasts dropped down in a colossal wave, howling and yelping with anticipation.

"*Yesss.*" Lechery coated the demon's hiss. "*Almost there, Franky.*"

Another step.

His heart raged in his chest, thumping against his sternum. All around, the room came to life, a living sea of black, sloshing with the beat of his pulse. The weight of the knife intensified, and he clutched it with all his might.

Another step.

"*Do it, Franky. Hurry. I can't survive another second within this dying vessel.*" The demon seethed. "*There's no more time.*"

Frank stopped, inches away from his daughter. He stood there for an eternity, watching the sparkle in her eyes. That smile. The innocence and joy radiating from her face. Her youthfulness. How could he tear that away from her? How could he steal her childhood and infect her with this virus, this disease?

But there was no turning back now, and he was no longer in control.

Against his will, he lifted the knife and pressed the blade against his wrist, feeling it slice through his skin, his veins, his tendons, like butter. The blood pooled around the steel's edge, clinging and seeping along its sides. And then it began to drip.

"*Feed her, Franky.*" The demon's eyes bulged with anticipation. "*Pour your life into her.*"

Chloe leaned forward, the smile vacating her face. Her lips parted, anxiously awaiting the crimson fluid to slather her throat.

"*Do it. Do it now, Franky. Finish this.*"

Frank's stare honed in on his daughter's open mouth, prepared for the end. With his fist clenched, Frank reached forward, drops weeping from the cut and sprinkling to the carpet below.

As his drops of life neared her waiting lips, a clamor erupted outside, causing him to freeze in place. The cacophony drowned out the primal cries from the shadows.

Thump, thump, thump.

His eyes widened with confusion, slowly drifting toward the front door. He watched, transfixed, as it pulsated with a series of shudders, a visual manifestation of the overwhelming sense of dread that hung in the air.

The demon's glare mirrored Frank's, taking in the door's repetitive tremble, as did its hundreds of malevolent pets. As the thumps ceased, it watched in horror as the locks barricading the safety of its den unlocked in unison. And then the front door swung open.

Bathed in the moon's glow, a woman emerged. A nurse. Donned in scrubs the color of midnight, she clutched a beaded string in her right hand, embellished with the emblem of The Lord. The cross dangled from her clenched fingers, and the intensity in her gaze conveyed a profound depth.

"Frank, stop!" Her command shattered the acute silence. "Don't do it!"

Shrinking away, the demon retreated from the sight, its menacing presence collapsing with each swing of the rosary. It was running out of time. "*No. No, no, no, no. You can't be here. You c an't!*"

"His strength is not a burden, but one which I carry willingly, demon." Emma's glare loomed on the beast, watching it buckle and break. With each passing breath, it seemed to shrink, losing its formidable grip. "And His glory will cast you away from this world and back into the depths."

The air grew thick with ambiguity and tension, stifling the room, until the demon countered with his own claim, turning its darting stare back to the father and daughter.

"*Do it, Franky. Do it before it's too late!*" Its voice had changed, no longer bearing the control and dominance it once carried. No, an eagerness lay in its words. These were pleas. An entity in need and at the end of its rope.

Frank's weary stare darted between his father's body and the woman standing at the door, unable to process his next move, his intentions. He was lost, in between realms.

Emma stepped into the room, rosary clutched in her out-stretched fist. "Don't move, Frank. It can no longer control you."

The demon recoiled, and a slithering incantation sprang from its black lips. It backpedaled away from the woman's ad-vance, its meandering sea of creatures following it—two waves retreating in fear and hate.

Clarity and understanding morphed in Frank's eyes as he took in the scene. With deliverance and creed, he withdrew his outstretched arm, watching as the drops of blood fell short of his daughter's lips.

Hisses and bellows of hate flung from the beast's wicked tongue, circling the room like a storm. A dead language not meant to be heard by mortal ears. The dim lights flickered, embers of hope dying only to be reborn a moment later.

In the chaos, Emma sprang forward, shedding all trepidation, and gripped the little girl by the hand. "Chloe! Chloe, can you hear me?" She knelt, staring into the young girl's lost eyes. "Do you remember me?"

A fogginess hovered within the girl's stare, conscious of her surroundings, yet not. Limbo. A dreamlike trance.

Not waiting for a response, Emma tugged on the girl's flaccid hand, pulling her away from the room's center. The two hud-dled together near the doorway, Emma's arms wrapped around Chloe's neck, shielding her with the doctrinal weapon dangling from her grasp.

"*No! Stop her!*" The demon wailed, its jaw unhinging into a morbid gape. The deafening screech reverberated through the apartment's foundation. A frenzied shake followed the tumultuous roar. Convulsions shot through the beast's core, followed by the virulent speech in the foreign, hoary tongue.

One after another, the shadows mustered an attack, talons and claws slicing through the air. But with each pass, the wispy soldiers burned away and sifted into the parched air. It was impossible to penetrate the numinous bubble Emma cast upon the room.

With unwavering determination, the nurse extended the rosary in front of her, its onyx beads glistening in the dim light. A surge of otherworldly energy coursed through her, filling the air with a faint, electric hum. "You... Can't... Have... Her!"

The demon's back arched, arms extended, claws cutting through the air. It roared again, an unsettling growl filled with the nightmares of the world. The boom sent cracks webbing across the walls and ceiling. A few nomadic sparks sang from within the breaks. The shadows splintered, hovering above their master and vacating the other areas of the room.

Frank came to his wits, and he blinked away the iniquitous chaos. He witnessed the disease enveloping the room, chunks of drywall and plaster falling to the ground. The tumult was relentless.

Emma held her ground, protecting the child with a fierce grip. A single prayer leaped from her mouth, aimed at the scourge and its fleeing wisps of black. The invocation repeated over and over, a series of strikes bludgeoning the beast with adherent fists.

With Chloe safely behind her, the nurse stepped forward, inching closer, watching the demon wither and balk at her advance. As she completed another revolution of the prayer, she stopped.

"You have no power over us, demon. Begone and return to the hellfire of your rancid birth! Begone! In Christ's name, begone!"

The whirling wisps, the cries, the shrieks, the thunderous rage from the shadows, all of it ceased. A serene calm settled over the room, broken only by the audible, labored breaths of Emma, serving as a reminder of her tangible existence.

The demon cowered, shielding its dead eyes from the cross pinning it against the wall. As its trembling hands shifted away from its face, its sight drifted from the nurse, landing on Frank.

"*Franky? Franky, please.*"

But it wasn't his father's voice or the carnal, deep articulation of the wraith. No, this was a voice Franky hadn't physically heard in years. Only in his dreams. A soothing sound that delivered a comforting slice of nostalgia.

Frank reeled as he listened to the voice beg for mercy. "M-Mikey?"

"*Please, brother.*" The weight of guilt pressed heavily on Franky's chest as Mikey's words pierced his heart. "*It was you. You orchestrated the deal, remember? You led the shooter into that very alley. My crimson blood stains your hands, Franky.*"

"No." In response to the accusations, Frank's head shook, expressing his disbelief. "That wasn't my fault."

"*You got me killed, Franky. Because of you, I'm gone. My bones lay in the ground because of you.*"

"That's not true."

His father's face softened, clearing the rage and hate from its features. Slowly, the black, lifeless eyes changed, making way for the sleepy gray of Mikey's that Frank had always found dignified. "*You let me die in that car, Franky. It's your fault. You couldn't help me then. Help me, now, brother!*"

"No . . . I didn't . . ." Frank stammered, unconvinced.

"*Denial will eat you alive, brother. What's done is done. But you can still fix this. Finish it. Do it for me, Franky. You owe me th at.*"

Frank's gaze lifted from the sunken old man skulking with deception to stare at the knife in his hand and the self-inflicted cut on his wrist. He watched as the meandering stream of red dripped down his arm, painting over the bruises and long-forgotten scars.

Was it my fault?

"*My baby boy. Please help me, son.*"

The soothing sound collected his attention once more, and he took in the source. His father's body still cringed before him, but femininity leaked from the edges. It was his mother's voice. An unforgettable stability he never imagined hearing again in this life. And it was beautiful, ushering in a wave of fondness and pleasantries, abandoned and buried.

"*You pushed me away, pushed your father into the arms of another woman. It was you, Franky. I need you to finish this. Do it for me, your mother.*"

"Frank, don't listen to it," Emma blurted, voice carrying with intent. "It lies, deceives, with gluttonous conviction! That's not your brother or your mother. It's not your father either. Listen to me, Frank."

The nurse came into his view, still proudly guarding his daughter from the room's evils. Her head wavered from side to side, urging him to stop and think, to unmask the facade which poisoned his mind.

His eyes twitched, and a darkness slowly blanketed him in its veil. He could feel his equilibrium breaking, accompanied by a layer of haze.

"*Franky*? *Please*!" His father squirmed, tears welling in his eyes. "*Help me*!"

He ignored the voice of his father, a slight wobble in his stance. He could feel the knife's cold handle in his fist. Craning his neck, he took in Emma and his daughter, hiding behind her. The eight-year-old no longer appeared entranced. A mask of fear now covered her features, and he knew what he had to do to stop the madness.

For a split fragment of time, Frank left this world. He left the darkness swirling around him. Bountiful light bathed him in hues of white and a voice, one full of hope and tranquility, broke through the blinding shine. It started as a whisper before blooming to a melodic tune.

"*The Lord's light will guide you through the darkness, Mister Collins*."

Kwame.

"*Nuru itashinda giza mchungaji wangu*." The voice lobbied. The blessing ricocheted through his skull, steering his next thought and action.

I know what I have to do now. I understand the meaning, he thought, feeling the words penetrate his soul.

He felt a warmth blossom from within, blanketing his body in zeal before the blinding radiance dimmed, dropping him back into the mania.

"*Franky, please!*" The demon seethed through clenched teeth, bringing Frank back. "*This body is spent! Time is our enemy!*"

As his sight drifted between his father's dying shell and his daughter, clarity dug its roots in, holding him firm. There was only one thing left to do. He had to end this for good.

"No, I won't help you," Frank muttered, never considering the demon with another look. "And you can't have my daughter."

Without another thought, he brought the blade to his throat. A swift slice, severing his jugular and carotid artery. Instantly, his flannel shirt filled with his life force, blooming with color before he collapsed to his knees.

"Frank! No!" Emma screeched, watching the blood spill from the gaping wound.

"*No!*" the demon's deafening bellow shattered the apartment's windows.

As Frank's limp body crashed to the floor, the clamorous boom fragmented the atmosphere, sending shock waves pulsing through the space. Chunks of drywall the size of trash cans fell from the ceiling and the walls collapsed, leaving mushrooms of dust spiraling into the rotting air.

Through the disarray and carnage, Emma fled, ducking under the sagging awning and dragging the eight-year-old out into the moonlight.

Once clear from the flying debris, they stood there, holding each other, eyes transfixed as the apartment's roof caved in. In a burst of heat, the apartment sparked to life, fires raging and engulfing the nefarious den in a fury. It scorched the remains, flaming tendrils reaching for the heavens and showering the neighborhood in a brilliant orange hue.

From within the fiery trenches and havoc, the infernal cries of a thousand souls shrilled into the cool spring night while wisps of blackness fluttered away like fragments of ash. Emma held Chloe close, watching as the apartment devoured itself and listening to the distant blare of a siren.

EPILOGUE

THE DINER

THE NEXT MORNING

The diner was bustling with the sound of dishes clattering, silverware tinkling, and the joyful hum of lighthearted conversations. A peaceful start to the new day for many breaking their fast, but not for them. A tense silence hung heavily around the two sitting alone in the booth. The back booth.

The nurse sat across from the young girl, a coffee mug warming her cupped hands. Wisps of aromatic steam sifted from the ceramic, bathing her in hazelnut's rejuvenating scent. Every few breaths, she stole glances at Chloe but hid them just as quickly. She had yet to learn how to paddle through these choppy waters.

As she brought the mug to her mouth, her mind wandered, looping back to the scene, to the carnage and death: the gluttonous shadows, the wraith, Frank. Deep down, she knew she had saved the girl's life. Possibly saved her soul from damnation, too, but an emptiness still ripped at her. Was it over? What happens now?

Fear and worry struck hard as she contemplated the effects of the previous night and their next page in this chapter. And now the weight of responsibility settled on her shoulders, like a burden she couldn't shake, even though she knew she wasn't the catalyst behind this mess. It was a curse.

She broke through the anxiety, a stare hovering on the stoic expression bleeding from the eight-year-old's face. Her eyes filled with a hint of sorrow as she struggled to conceal her longing to connect with the young girl, to comfort her, and to help her through this. Burying the apprehension, she called out, her voice soft and filled with a maternal quality that was foreign to her ears. "Chloe?"

Silence.

"Chloe?" Emma shifted forward on the polyester cushion. "Can you hear me, child?"

The young girl's unblinking gaze remained fixed through the two glass panes on her left as if trapped in a catatonic state. She was still somewhere else, just like the previous eight hours—in between realms. She didn't even notice the small bird hopping around outside one pane.

After Emma had rushed her away from the blazing apartment fire, Chloe shut down—a reclusive mute, withdrawn and disengaged from the harsh reality her eyes revealed to her. She wouldn't even respond when spoken to. Speech fell on deaf ears as the young girl maintained her distant gaze, avoiding any direct eye contact. An internal escape mechanism to protect her mind from the brutal truth.

Emma released a sigh, knowing her attempts were asinine. Her stare drifted out the same window, watching the graceful hues of sunrise extinguishing the night. They had escaped death's grip, but she found no comfort in that. A whole new map lay before her, and now, she had to figure out how to navigate it.

A yawn followed the sigh as she stared out into the world, scanning the parking lot, the newly budded maples lining the sidewalk. She was exhausted and running on fumes. Fatigue took root the second she slid into the seat, marching alongside worry's merciless nagging. She could feel the heaviness in her eyes and the weight of draining emotions dragging her down. However, she couldn't afford to rest, even though her body and mind desperately craved it. She needed to think, to plan, without the crushing weight of debilitation.

The coffee's engines were still sputtering to life, and she desperately needed some energy. Maybe a walk would help? A splash of cold water on her face? Anything to get the cylinders pumping again.

The waitress who seated them approached seconds later, a decanter sloshing with a fresh batch of caffeine firmly gripped in her right hand. She was probably in her mid-forties, from what Emma could tell, based on her looks: wisps of gray weaving through her full head of black hair and the soft wrinkles lining her eyes and lips. The woman's charisma was contagious, and either she played the role well, or she enjoyed this line of work.

After topping off Emma's mug, the waitress's attention drifted to Chloe. Her eyes softened, a hint of concern swirling within the green. "Are you still thinking about what you want, kiddo? Some juice, some milk?"

There wasn't a response. Chloe held her emotionless glare.

"Can you bring her an apple juice, please?" Emma asked, forcing the smile that normally came so naturally. "She's a little shy around settings like this. But I'm sure she'll come around with a taste of nature."

"Of course, not a problem. I'll be right back with that and to get your orders." As the waitress turned to leave, the coffee pot locked in her fist, Emma called out, stopping her in the middle of the pivot, "Excuse me, miss." Emma left the comforts of the bench and stood, rounding the table and nearing the waiting diner worker. "Just a second real quick."

"Yeah. Do you need anything else?"

Emma strolled forward, nearing the woman without invading her space. A split-second glance at Chloe was all she allowed herself before turning her attention back to the waitress. "Miss, can you do me a favor? I'm going to use the restroom. Two minutes tops, but can you make sure she's okay while I'm gone? She gets really—"

"Nervous, right?" The waitress finished the sentence. "I can sense that from her. Poor little thing. Kids usually radiate around me, but that one . . ." Empathy accompanied her words. "What do you think triggered her shyness? If you don't mind me asking."

Emma stiffened at the question but worked through the nerves and thoughts. "She's uh . . . she's just always been this way. Since birth, reserved and quiet. Kept to herself, you know?"

"Oh, I know the type, dear. My husband paints that picture well." A snicker leaked from her mouth. "He'd rather stick his face in a book than hold a conversation. But I guess that's the world of extremes, right? My world's full of laughter and emotion, whereas his is serene and tranquil."

Emma agreed with the statement, a grin and nod aimed the waitress's way. "Opposites attract, right?"

"Indeed, they do."

"Well, thank you, miss." Emma's eyes shot past the waitress, eyeing the sign pinned on the diner's far wall that read *Restrooms*. An arrow below the word pointed down a hall she'd noticed when they entered earlier. "I'll be right back, but if you could just take a look here and there? Just make sure she's okay?"

"Not a problem. Take your time and I'll grab the apple juice. Maybe the sight will chisel away at the wall she's built." The waitress ended the speech with another one of her radiant smiles.

Emma wondered if she could genuinely mirror that look now that everything had turned upside down. She had her doubts.

"Thank you again,"—Emma's eyes darted to the name badge pinned to the waitress's shirt— "Cindy. I appreciate it."

"Not a problem, sweetie. I'll be right back."

2

Beads of water dropped from her chin and nose, falling into the sink's basin. The hydration released a sense of focus while she stood there, fixated on the woman in the mirror. She stared at her reflection, watching the droplets pool into streams and meander down her face. A lazy river eroding the banks before plunging from the crag.

But her focus wasn't only on the cool water she splashed upon her skin. The woman she took in looked haggard, distraught. A poor example of the caregiver patients asked for and loved. Her glasses sat on a shelf to her left, so she leaned in, exploring this stranger's features. The skin tone wasn't right (a brackish gray hue) and dark circles blotched the underside of her eyes, revealing a subject a decade older. The crevices loitering at her eyes' corners and lips appeared deeper, too, more advanced than a thirty-eight-year-old.

Blowing out a breath, she wiped the remnants of water away with her palms and shook off the thoughts and images swirling in her mind. After drying her hands with a towel, she repositioned her glasses and reached into her purse. Her hand came away with a small orange bottle. She held it up to the artificial light hanging from the ceiling, reading the label—*fluoxetine-Prozac*—before twisting off the lid. Her psychiatrist prescribed the medication weeks ago, and she had always dismissed the thought of taking antidepressants. She was very familiar with the horror stories of addiction and dependency, but that fear was moot. She didn't think she needed them; however, maybe the pills would help her cope with what she had seen the night before? Maybe they would soften the pain and stress? It was worth trying.

One blue and white capsule fell into her waiting palm, and she tossed it back without another thought. As she turned away from the mirror, she already felt like her wounds were healing. It was a long, painful night. One which would haunt her for eternity. But she needed to get back to Chloe and piece together what lay ahead for both of them.

As Emma rounded the hall, the diner's voice rushed in, swallowing her ears. A family of four (they appeared to be your classic family) sat at a square table on her left. The mother and father contemplated the options on the menu, reading the specials while the son, the older of the two children, sulked in his chair, clearly annoyed by his participation in this endeavor. The daughter, a year or two younger than Chloe, colored on the white kids' menu given to her. She sang lyrics to a pop song in an undertone, hushed voice.

Strolling forward, Emma glanced at an elderly couple sitting in a booth much like theirs on her right. The man wore a brown fedora, shielding his bright blue eyes, while the woman, giddy and plump, sported a flowery patterned sundress. The petals' vibrant colors (blue and yellow) mimicked her personality and glow. A pleasantry resonated in both of their words as they engaged. A lifetime of partnership and love. As she passed by, the two carried on a carefree conversation while sipping their tea.

Waiters, waitresses, and busboys bustled around, serving, chatting with patrons, cleaning and clearing tables. A frenzied dance. The scene felt so natural, so normal. Listening to the world eased the pull on her heart. Good still flowed freely, filling the souls of this establishment with raw emotions. And it almost brought a smile to her mouth.

As her stare drifted to the back booth, praying the apple juice had awakened Chloe from her mental paralysis, shock barreled into her, kicking down the door. A large man stood next to their booth, his hands resting on the table. His mouth moved, accompanied by a friendly grin.

She approached with caution, watching as the man contin-ued his small talk directed at the bench where the child sat.

Who is that, and why is he talking to Chloe?

Once in earshot, she could hear the man's words. An accent rode along with his speech, one full of hope and understanding, and the enunciations carried no sign of danger. A sereneness was layered upon every syllable, yet, after the horrors of the previous night, she wasn't about to let anyone near the young girl.

"Excuse me." She prodded forward, forcing the man to end his gentle lean against the table and take a step back. "Can I help you with something?" The inquiry lacked friendliness.

She glanced Chloe's way, noticing the girl no longer stared absently out the window. In fact, that blankness, that void, had faded from her face. Hints of color threatened to pulse from the eight-year-old's skin once more.

A toothy smile formed, and the man's eyes softened. "Hello there. You must be her mother."

Emma glared his way, eyes hovering over his features, his dark skin, his attire. He wore medical scrubs, navy blue, much like the ones she regularly wore. "Why are you speaking to her?"

The man's light brown eyes lifted to the ceiling, and a flutter pulsed through his gestures. "Forgive me, miss. My apologies." His thick arms raised from his sides, palms touching in prayer. "If I have offended you, I am truly sorry."

She could feel the palpable honesty and genuineness emanat-ing from him, like a gentle breeze caressing her senses. The air was charged with an unmistakable aura, creating an atmosphere of trust and ease. Despite their unfamiliarity and his breach of social boundaries with his small talk, she found herself at ease in his presence.

"I'm just wondering why you're talking to her. Do you know her or something?" Her response was lighter, not blazoned with the prickly thorns from before.

The man's hands came to rest on his wide stomach, and a twinkle sparked in his eyes. "No. The girl is new to me, but I gravitate to those in need. I am prone to it. A weakness of mine. Perhaps that is why this profession called upon me."

"You help people? A caregiver, a . . . nurse?"

"Indeed." He paused, his look loitering over her for a moment. Longer than deemed appropriate. "I sense that is why you are a health practitioner as well."

Emma's head cocked, surveying his eyes. "How did you know that?"

The corners of his mouth curled, revealing soft dimples in his round cheeks she hadn't noticed before. "You can always tell. The ones who give, serve. They cast off their essence in very unique ways and patterns."

He let the statement sink in as he continued to study her. "Your essence, for example, spirals and it soars high amongst the heavens. It carries something too. A burden? Unfortunately, I cannot see it clearly."

She listened to his words, feeling the dread and anguish slip away. A peaceful tranquility bathed her being while she stood there, almost forgetting about the past.

"Again, I apologize for the offense, miss," the man continued. "But the young one seemed to be in pain as I passed by, and I cannot help myself when a lamb is wounded."

Emma stole a look at Chloe, seeing something in her eyes she thought was dead and rotting. A warmth also resonated there, just below the surface, inching to rupture and crawl out into the world.

With her attention redirected at the large nurse, she answered, "It's . . . uh, fine. I just don't like her speaking with strangers. I may be old-fashioned, but she's my responsibility and I have to care for her."

"From what I can tell,"—that sparkle twinkling in his eyes brightened—"you are excelling at your role, miss. I applaud your efforts. Many mothers in this world are unfit and incapable, but it is clear you are one that nurtures, guards."

"Thank you, but I'm not her . . ." Emma trailed off, holding on to that last word. She thought about it, what it meant. She wasn't the girl's mother, nor even a family member, but what this child needed the most in the world right now was love and protection. Both could be delivered as they sorted through this mess.

"Thank you for the kind words, sir. I appreciate it." She could hear Chloe shuffling around on the bench behind her. "She was feeling ill, but whatever you said to her seemed to brighten her spirits. Thank you."

"Oh, it is my pleasure, miss." The large nurse raised his hands once more in prayer, aimed at both Emma and Chloe. "I pray for you and your blessed one. *Nuru itashinda giza mchungaji mangu.*"

The blessing looped in Emma's mind, an orchestra of violins and cellos washing away the lingering thoughts. It delivered a spark, reigniting her burning flame.

"What does it mean?" her soft voice asked, feeling the lather rinse away.

"You will discover that soon, miss." He stepped forward and embraced her with a gentle touch, his hand slightly caressing her shoulder. A sensation sat there, warming her collarbone, and it lingered long after he withdrew.

"When your time comes, *you* will know what the words mean." His chin dropped as he nodded her way.

A weightlessness sank into her as she listened, watching the radiance of his smile, the innocence behind the missing tooth in his lower jaw, his casual yet warming words. An angelic quality loomed around the man, a gift to this world and to all.

"I understand. Thank you," Emma stated, almost enveloped in the man's hypnotic aura.

"Blessings to you both, miss." The man delivered another nod and smiled at Chloe as he leaned over the table. "Hopefully, our paths will cross again."

"I hope so too." The phrase leaked off Emma's tongue without even thinking. "What . . . what is your name, sir? If you don't mind me asking."

"My name is Kwame. A shepherd amongst the sheep." With that, the man turned and walked away, leaving the two in the empty booth.

Emma watched as the man's frame disappeared through the diner's glass door. She stood there, eyes fixed on the entrance, wondering about the encounter, wondering about the prayer, wondering what to do next.

But something else crept into her thoughts now that Kwame was absent. Feelings, rather, of vulnerability, despair, and loneliness. That pure tranquility he bled throughout the diner drowned the second he exited, and a sense of dread and foreboding rushed in. She felt a panic attack coming on and questioned whether the blue and white capsules had dispersed into her system yet. Did she take enough, or did she need more already?

"Look, Emma."

The voice broke her away from the consternation, and her shaky eyes fell on the eight-year-old. The young girl had slid over to the window, energy and charisma purring from her voice.

"What is it, Chloe?" Emma scooted onto the bench, feeling her heart rate slow. Her stare hovered out the window, trying to catch a glimpse of whatever excitement enticed the girl. "What do you see?"

"It's a birdie. See?" Chloe glanced over her shoulder, excitement strapped in every fidgety movement. "See?"

Emma shifted on the bench, sliding beside the enthusiastic girl. "Where?"

Chloe pointed to the window sill, eyes glued downward through the dual layers of glass. "There. It's right there, Emma. Look."

Emma mirrored the gaze, feeling the child's warmth radiate off her cheeks. There, standing on the sill, was a small bird. The same small bird from earlier. A finch. A piece of dried grass hung from its yellow beak.

"Yeah, look at that." Emma smiled, thinking this moment was a start. The start to many more loving moments. It felt natural. She could do this. She could care for this child, raise her as her own. Frank would appreciate that. "I see it, Chloe. It's cute, huh?"

"So cute and so little."

Emma didn't respond. She didn't need to. This instance, this moment, was all she needed. She felt happy and whatever blessing Kwame said to the girl brought out her happiness too.

The two stared at the bird for several breaths, watching it hop around the wooden sill, wallowing in the pristine morning rays until . . .

A flash of gray scrambled the heart-wrenching scene, followed by claws and teeth. It was fast, a surprising blur in their shaken view. As they recovered from the instant recoil, their eyes landed on the root of evil: a cat. A gray tabby sat upon the sill, proudly holding the bird in its mouth. Feathers floated around it in the morning air, fluttering down like snowflakes. The feline's eyes stared back at the woman and child, holding menace and violence in its glare. The eyes of a serpent, slivers of black breaking the bold bands of yellow.

But then the uncanny occurred. The feline slowly blinked both eyes in unison. A slow, deliberate, dramatic act for the two spectators. As they reopened, the hypnotizing color was gone, leaving nothingness in its wake. Pure blackness lived there, void of anything else. Void of life and good.

"Max?" Chloe asked before watching the cat leap from the perch and vanish from sight. "Was that Max?"

Emma buckled in the seat without answering. Her mind spun, collapsing on the hinges of reality while her thoughts were devoured by a wave of darkness coming at her from every direction. Its rotten tendrils slithered along her skin, impregnating the warmth and hope that once lived there. She could sense a presence surrounding her, hiding in the shadows.

And then came the whispers.

ACKNOWLEDGEMENTS

There are so many special people that played a part in this project.

Foremost, I need to acknowledge my late father, Merrill Gibbs Arnold (Pops). Since he slipped away from us back in 2019, not a single day has gone by without him occupying my thoughts.

I also want to thank my beautiful, loving wife, Tara. I want you to know that I truly appreciate your patience while I create these tales.

I can't forget my four littles: Emma, Aubrey, Aria, and Luke. Thank you for keeping me on my toes. Love you guys.

To my secondary kin, the Lopez family, thank you for always being supportive, listening to my ideas, and always showing unconditional love.

Thank you Dani Yeager at Hack and Slash Editing, my incredible editor. You cleaned up my mess with expertise and an uncanny crispness. All I can say is 'wow.'

Finally, I need to thank a few fellow authors who I deeply respect and admire. Thank you A.G. Mock and Chad Miller. You've always been willing to lend advice and steer me in a productive direction. You guys rock.

ABOUT THE AUTHOR

From an early age, J.B. knew he could create mind-blowing, emotionally charged stories filled with enigmatic characters and story arcs. Fond, nostalgic memories still loop in his mind about the three or four-page thrillers he wrote in middle-school for his friends. Around the same time, he discovered Stephen King and Dean Koontz. Both prolific writers influenced his creativity and helped hone his love for the craft. But the love remained dormant for years.

In the early stages of the Covid pandemic, JB's genuine passion came to fruition. Now happily married and a father, his inspiration bloomed after hearing his second daughter's desire to write a novella. Day after day, the two sat at the kitchen table, exchanging ideas, creating treacherous villains, and building a majestic fantasy world through the use of a pen. He was hooked, and the passion to write came rushing back like an avalanche.

Since then, he has completed three manuscripts: The Streets of Floria, Exit 202, and A Shadow's Wraith. You can also find his numerous short stories published through online magazines and websites. His current work in progress (WIP) titled The Chronicles of Barbasos, is an anthology of shorts, due out early 2025.

JB lives in sunny California with his wife and four children; three daughters and a son. Oh, and there's his writing partner; his gray tabby, Max. When he isn't writing, he loves to read, play golf, and listen to 80s rock and 90s metal.

Visit **jbarnold-author.com** for updates and future projects.

THE CHRONICLES OF BARBASOS

13 tales of crime, debauchery, and sin

COMING EARLY 2025

J B ARNOLD

THE HOLLIER HOUSE

AN EXCERPT FROM THE CHRONICLES OF BARBASOS

Adeline's Story

The hearth's warmth radiated throughout the parlour; a beckoning for clients new and old. Yet, this night was quiet. Two sailors, chipper and reeking of wine, had sauntered in earlier. But the memory of their presence faded once they ascended the plush stairs to the boarding rooms. Only the sparse, lascivious moans from beyond the landing reminded Adeline they weren't a part of a dream.

The young girl sat there, slouched in a high-back, red velvet chair. Her long, lean legs dangling over the right armrest. Boredom had festered in, and she picked at a black tuft, watching how the leather slowly peeled away. Most evenings, she ran about completing her tasks, leaving no time to think. Her duties were simple: rushing about and refilling cups, delivering clean towels, removing soiled bedding. But the need didn't present itself this evening.

During the last turn, she expected her role in the brothel to increase, perhaps to take on a younger client or two, but rules are rules. And the house procurer, Madam Hollier, was a stickler. Not to mention petty. Once a girl reached thirteen turns, it deemed her ready. A plum ready to pluck. Yet, Adeline sat there, knowing it would be four moons before she reached the ripe age.

A thud shuddered from the room above her head. The moans returned as well. Her sight drifted up, watching flakes of plaster and dust fall lazily in the stale air. Chewing on her bottom lip, she focused on the sounds coming from the room, listening, learning. Her older sister's lustful groans signalled the end was near. It also signalled a return to her duties. Based on the climatic display, collecting all the girl's attention, Scarlett's room would need a full linen change.

As she flung her legs off the armrest, a client sauntered through the swinging doors, taking swift strides. He was tall with a lean build, and confidence dripped from every pore. His shoulder-length blonde locks bounced with each step. He wasn't a regular, but this wasn't his maiden voyage inside Hollier's House, either. Adeline recognized him and had heard whispers from the other girls, too.

The man ignored the few girls loitering near the entrance, deaf ears to their flirtatious cat-calls. He carved a determined path for the Madam's book room, clutching a satchel made of fine cloth. He entered the room uninvited and closed the door.

Adeline and the others stilled, whispers snuffed as their eyes gleamed at the shut door. Their minds teetered with thoughts from the man's bold gesture. Some worried about the brashness, others, the more experienced, viewed this as an opportunity. Either way, something was happening. Perhaps something with financial implications.

Madam Hollier sat at a bistro table, legs crossed. A quill and parchment lay before her, and a half-full flute of white wine rested in her delicate grasp. She remained silent as the man entered, watching him with indictable eyes. She ignored his assertiveness, waiting for his righteousness to display.

Ignoring pleasantries or permission, the man pulled out the second chair, and sat across from her. He laid the satchel down, covering her parchment. His gaze hovered over her form, following the many layers of fabric covering her legs upward to the tight bodice. His leer hung for a moment, taking in her voluptuousness, before finally meeting her eyes.

"Madam, it has been too long, my old friend." His lips curled, exposing a sly smile. "How is business?"

She ignored the empty greeting and question, drilling holes through his emerald eyes. "You should not have returned. Your last visit, your *mess,* and the reverberations still linger in these halls."

He leaned forward, hands coming together, fingertips touching. "Mess?" The word slithered off his tongue. "I'm sure you're mistaken, Madam. Unless you refer to a few soiled sheets?"

"A man's seed washes away with a scrub." Her eyes narrowed. "The crimson red of life does not."

"I paid for the service, as I always have." A breath blew from his lips as he dismissed her claim with a wrist's flick, eyes rolling. "Besides, she enjoyed our little romp." His eyebrow raised. "Even the rough parts."

"You shattered Eira's arm and raped her of her beauty. Her scars have barely healed. Every time she glances into the looking glass, fresh tears flow. A river of diffidence." She paused, letting the words grip like a vise. "She was a prized acquisition, that one. Brought over from Opal two turns ago. Now, I'm lucky to get any return for my efforts. No one wants her with the scars."

The grin slowly left his lips, listening to her loose allegations. He leaned back, posture stiffening. "Be mindful of your tongue, woman. Our arrangement is very . . . *profitable* for you. I know you grow fond of your assets, maybe even care for them, but don't forget, they're just cattle. Prey for the wolves of this magnificent city. And as you know," he paused, making sure his words penetrated deeply. "I have an exquisite palate that caters to a certain cuisine."

Fire raged within her stare, and her aspect sang with rigidness. "I am well aware of the coins you drop in my house, Elric." Her words were calm, yet assertive, as she placed the wineglass down. "And I am equally aware of your lustful desires."

"Madam?" He paused again, open hand gesturing towards his chest. "Your words wound me. But perhaps they hold a span or merit." The slick grin morphed once more, eyes flickering with motivation. "But enough of your pettiness." He reached into the bag, removing a fistful of shiny silvers. "I'm here for business and *pleasure*, love."

Her eyes flashed to the bounty Elric held, attempting to hold in the rapacious greed. Despite its prosperity, the Hollier House failed to provide lasting comfort. Madam Hollier's generosity extended to her girls, of course, fancying them in silks and satins. She even kept them fed by bringing in local masters skilled in a myriad of culinary arts. But under the chandelier's flames, Elric held something that could procure the future.

The detest brewing in her gaze faded, and her cheeks flushed with new life. "Well then, Elric, my dear friend. Let us put the past behind us." Her lips mirrored Elric's, curling up into a covetous grin. "How can I tempt thee? A Leumerian beauty, a pair of locals, or one of my finest? If I am not mistaken, Jade is available, and according to her lengthy list of suitors, she *always* delivers."

He held her eyes, observing how rapidly her body language and gestures changed. That rigid, indignant stare retreated, revealing the soft features she flaunted when arranging transactions. This was the madam he sought, the one he knew he could buy. The one with the ability to gift-wrap and hand-deliver a particular fantasy. From an early age, Elric learned how to control people, influence them with his father's wealth. His alliance with Drake, the city's crime lord, only magnified his hold on others. Both made him feel entitled, exclusive to the daily scum of this city. And he could see his power blooming.

He leaned back, slowly dropping the coins onto the iron table. Each one delivered a rhythmic *clang* as it struck the forged metal. He watched her eyes flutter to the growing mound before racing back; her grin widening.

"As tempting as that sounds, dear, I must decline." He reached down and picked up a coin with his thumb and index finger, rolling it with his smooth, unblemished fingertip. "Tonight is a special occasion, and your everyday slop will not suffice. I am yearning for something different, unexplored, untainted. Something that will scratch this festering itch."

"Ahh," hues of pink flushed her fair skin. "Your appetite and cravings certainly are expanding, my friend."

"Well, what can I say? Travelling beyond the Green Sea and savouring all its delicacies has piqued my inclination for new and exotic cuisines." A pause ensued as he took her form once more, his eyes exploring her curves. "Elegance surrounds me now, and I always get what I want. Understand, Madam Hollier?"

Silence ensued as she watched him, cogs spinning with gluttonous intent. Over the years, she had mastered this facade, this masked display of deceit. She would play his game, fancy his wishes, and reap the benefits. Her house needed it.

"I think I may have a solution to tame the fire looming, Elric. And you may have seen her outside in the parlour." Her eyes drifted to the closed door behind him. "I rarely offer such a gift based on my own instilled morals, but you have swayed me. She is young, innocent, and . . . as you have requested, untouched."

Elric raised an eyebrow, craning his neck and glancing over his shoulder at the door. His mind wandered, envisioning the girl: her soft features, her trembling limbs as his finger caressed her youthful skin. The inexperience, the naiveness. The thoughts sparked the flame, arousal igniting the blazing fury.

As he turned and faced the madam, he asked one simple question. "What is her name?"

She held her tongue for several breaths, allowing the anxiousness to peak before answering with a single word. "Adeline."

In the parlour, the older girls crept toward the closed door, bare feet tip-toeing across the polished stone. But their efforts fell short, and they scattered quickly, like nocturnal pests, when the door handle turned.

With the door arched open, Elric stood there, satchel hanging from his shoulder. His fingers latched onto the doorframe's sides. His sight swept the room and all its splendour. He ignored the older girls sprawled out on chairs and sofas, staring at him like he was a god. He even bypassed those leaning against the parlour's walls, not giving them a second glance. But his stare narrowed and focused once he saw the young girl sitting in the high-back chair near the room's back. He knew who she was.

Adeline.

Slowly, an eager grin morphed, displaying his true intentions as he locked eyes with her. Without haste, he released his grip on the doorframe and strolled forward, never breaking the gaze. Within breaths, he stood before her, admiring her smooth, ivory skin and deep blue eyes, captivated by her mousy hair, and light freckles. Both remained silent, but through the deafening silence, the message was obvious.

A slight shudder flowed through Adeline as she sat there, staring up at this beautiful stranger. As she collapsed into his charming, emerald eyes, she realised this was *her* moment, her opportunity to show the others she was ready; prepared to become a woman.

As her heart hammered, a call from the madam's book room broke the euphoric moment. "Sabine. Enter at once, dear."

Adeline dropped her alluring gaze and peered around Elric, watching an older girl leap from her sofa and hustle towards the room on nimble, bare feet. With Scarlett occupied upstairs, Sabine claimed the role of most experienced, and thus, most trusted.

Adeline's eyes followed the older girl as she entered the room, the door swinging open and then settling in a position that allowed muffled whispers to escape. Straining to hear a word, Adeline's ears perked to listen to the conversation, but she ended up disappointed and empty-handed.

Why does she want Sabine? This is my time, not hers. It's clear he wants me. She thought.

During her three turns in the Hollier House, Adeline observed the madam pulling a select few to her. And she always wondered what the whispers entailed. The hushed tongues were compelling, and she yearned to know the truth; the secrets they shared. Deep down, she prayed that someday the madam would confide in her, too.

Feeling Elric's eyes still fixed on her, her sight fluttered back to the man. Through the anxiety and confusion, she attempted a sinful smile to return the enticement, freckled cheeks flushed. Even with Sabine summoned, she could still court him. Maybe woo the man. Before she could open her mouth to greet him, the madam called out once more.

"Adeline. Come, now, girl."

Her view drifted to the madam's chambers once more, frustration apparent in her features.

Why is she calling me now? What's happening?

Her lean neck stretched to the side, watching Sabine exit the madam's room. The older, more experienced, girl strolled forward, her stare locked on Elric. Without thinking, Adeline stood and wavered towards the room on nervous, quaking knees. As the two passed each other, Sabine glanced over and puckered her lips, blowing a mocking kiss before continuing her short trek.

Adeline slowed and watched Sabine's flirtatious strides. Of all the house's experienced girls, Sabine had the best walk, the most seductive. Before this moment, Adeline enjoyed watching Sabine, studying her motion: the swaying hips, the sexuality oozing from her. But as she watched now, the only feeling conveyed was jealousy. This wasn't fair. It was clear the blonde man had chosen her, so why was the madam sending Sabine?

She stopped and turned as Sabine gently gripped Elric's hand and whispered in his ear. The two shared a playful giggle before the older girl pulled him away, leading him toward the stairs.

"Adeline! Now!"

The command shook her, bringing her back. Confusion warped her mind, but she also could feel the detest percolating from being passed over. But sulking had to be delayed. If she was to prove her worth. She needed strength, assertiveness, and needed to move forward. The madam demanded her presence, and perhaps she could still contribute in some capacity; justify her relevance.

Adeline buried the ill feelings and trudged towards the open door, feeling the butterflies flutter in her gut. A summoning had only occurred when others her age were in tow. She didn't know what to expect, but deep in her thoughts, she prayed for good omens.

She stood in the open doorway, feeling the nerves shutter in each extremity. Since arriving in Barbasos three turns prior, the only soul that lobbied her an ounce of dignity was the madam. The other girls in the house teased her, mocked her efforts and looks, but the madam never did. The house procurer was the closest thing to a mother Adeline could label.

"Yes, my lady," she muttered, hearing the scoffs and giggles behind her.

The madam stopped stacking the silvers that lay before her and glanced Adeline's way. "Come inside, girl, and close the door." With a sense of purpose, her eyes widened and a spark of anticipation flickered within them. "I have a proposition for you."

Sabine led Elric upstairs, gentle, playful tugs on his hand. Every few steps, she looked back over her shoulder, a contagious, alluring grin strapped to her lips. She understood her role here, knew the preparations needed. She was one of the few the madam trusted, and competency was her specialty.

Once on the landing, her pace quickened, pulling him faster down the hall. His eyes darted to the right, staring at the series of closed doors they passed, wondering what depraved fantasies lay hidden within. He also kept wondering when they would present Adeline to him. Was this older girl an appetiser before dessert? He expected perfection for the hefty bounty he paid. Slowly, his sight shifted back to Sabine, fueled by the young woman's sinful looks.

The room at the end with the red door was off-limits most nights. Saved for privileged, voracious clients willing to drop a moon's wage. Elric fit the bill, given his satchel was much lighter now, yet not drained.

Sage and vanilla filled his nose as Sabine unlocked the door with a brass key hidden within her bosom. With a simple twist, she opened the room and all its plushness. As they walked through the entrance, Elric spun around, taking in the improvident sights. A large, feathered mattress lay centred in the room, adorned with a hand-carved mahogany head and footboard. Fluffed white pillows rose in height, blanketing much of the elegant piece. Cast-iron candelabras, taller than a child, stood guard on the room's sides; vibrant light flickering to a rhythmic beat. The room was an empty canvas, craving a masterpiece.

As Elric continued his visual appraisal, Sabine stepped forward, halting the man's fluid, apathetic motion.

"She'll be up soon, love. Try to relax while I prepare you for bliss." The words left her lips in an erotic whisper.

Showing authority, she pressed herself against his body, hands cupping his freshly shaven face. She gazed up at him, seeing his lustful desire blossom. With her body so close, she could also feel it in his loins. She was here for entertainment as the opening act for this orchestra.

With a playful push to his chest, Elric fell backwards, landing in the fluff of feathers and satin, feet pinned to the floor. He laid there on his back, staring at Sabine, watching her seductive leer. Her role in this fantasy was clear now. She was there to tease him, stimulate and seduce him. Bring the smouldering water to a boil before the eruption. And he liked it.

With precision, Sabine crawled onto the bed and straddled him; knees drowning in the deep mattress. She peered down at him, watching him flutter with excitement. As she leaned closer, she whispered into his ear, hot breath tickling his cheek. "Hold still, now. She'll love the idea of being in control."

After grinding forward with her hips, she reached out and grasped his left wrist, caressing the skin. She leaned that direction, laying his hand near the edge of the mattress. Smoothly, she broke her gentle grip and found the two strips of silk sewed into the fabric. With nimble, soft fingers, she wrapped the strips around his wrist, finishing the bind with a simple knot.

He sat up, resting on his elbow, and wrapped his free fingers around her tiny waist. "What is this? Some sort of game?" His eyes flickered with delight. "Is this what you meant by control?"

"Just relax, love. She's clean and pure." Her eyes bore down on him with seduction, assuring the fantasy was in its infancy. "Let her explore, discover, and learn. It'll be worth it."

That slick grin came back as he laid back down, nodding in approval. The anxiousness of the moment was escalating, fueling the scorching fire. He was ready now, but he would allow Adeline to take her time. Not for long, though. He bought the girl, paid in full. And he would play with his new toy, however he felt fit.

With a deeper grind of her hips, she leaned to the right, tying his free wrist in a matching knot just as Madam Hollier had instructed. She tested his confinement and then reached back into her bosom, pulling out a strand of red satin.

"What's that for? Need to tie up my ankles, too?" He asked, coyness etched in each word.

"No, no, no, love." She licked her upper lip, arching an eyebrow. "She's very young, innocent. And unfortunately, nervous about this magical encounter. Even with her nerves, she's very excited to please you. To give *you,* her gift."

He thought about the statement for a few heartbeats, envisioning his new plaything straddling him, thrusting down on his sleek flesh. Slowly, his mind morphed Sabine's delicate face, replacing it with Adeline's; the freckles, the loose, mousy hair, the scent of youth. He could almost feel her trembling flesh pressed against his, her stuttering, nervous speech as she tried to play the part.

Sabine could see his eyes fill with euphoria, signalling the next explicit instruction. "It's a blindfold, love. You should wear it in the beginning. Just until she is comfortable, though."

The thought of not seeing Adeline didn't fuel his urges, but he understood this game. And he was ready to play. He would wear the mask, allow her to learn the ropes and build confidence, explore his body before he took control. He didn't respond to the suggestion, allowing her to cover his eyes with the strip of fabric, tying it behind his head. The red hues suffocated his sight, but a presence still lingered in the room.

Sabine slid backwards off the bed. He lifted his head, shifting it right and left, listening to the subtle sounds of the room: the flickering of candle flame, Sabine's light footsteps as she backpedalled away from the bed, her intoxicating breathing. He could feel her piercing eyes on him through the veil of intimacy.

He grew bored of the games, the teasing. Staleness smothered them. "Bring me the girl." The words were forceful, demanding.

"I'm on my way, love. Your prize will be here shortly," she countered, making her way to the door.

Elric's ears perked, catching the faint sound of Sabine's footsteps before the red door creaked open and closed. Moments passed, leaving him with his lustful thoughts and visions. He laid there impatiently, anticipation swelling like a reservoir on the brink of rupture.

Why is it taking so long?

He assumed Adeline was as nervous as Sabine suggested, but the young girl belonged to him now. In his position of authority, he established the rules, exercised his autonomy, and eventually grew weary of waiting. As he was about to yank his bound wrists free and tear away the blindfold, a sound echoed from outside the room. Hushed voices before the door opened with a grinding screech.

Bare feet tiptoeing on the wooden floor commanded Elric's attention after the door shut. They encroached the bed, then split into two parties; left and right. Or was there a third pair standing in front? He wasn't sure. Was that a muffled giggle? It didn't matter. The wait was over.

Excitement pervaded the room as he laid there, knowing the moment was close. Sabine had returned with the girl, and that lingering, erotic feeling of being watched resurfaced. Sabine outperformed her duties, and now she would stay and experience the climatic ending to this saga. Maybe even take part in the escapades at some point. He could only hope.

"Come here, girl." He shifted back on the bed, adjusting his position and bowing his legs apart. "I shan't bite."

She stood at the end of the bed, a slight shake to her stance. She remained silent but subdued to his bidding. Elric could sense Sabine urging her along, encouraging her with gestures and soft whispers.

A knee penetrated the thick plush mattress, followed by another. Despite her weight being more than expected, the girl was still petite and ripe for the plucking. Elric felt her gentle touch as she crawled forward, legs straddling his lap. As her delicate fingers traced his cheek, the soothing scent of lavender filled the air, lingering as they moved down to rest on his chest. He resisted the urge to break free from the straps and take her. She needed time before the beast sprang.

Her nimble fingers went to work, removing the satchel from around his neck before unbuttoning his shirt. With his shirt strewn open, she leaned down, hot breath leaving a wake of goosebumps on his flesh. A shudder flew through his limbs, but he loved this. It was intoxicating, euphoric.

Slowly, the girl caressed his chest, inching forward, nearing his face. She leaned to the right and whispered into his ear. "Are you ready?"

A sensual moan slid between his clenched teeth upon hearing her voice. "Yes. Yes." The straps around his wrists grew taut as he pulled, but he controlled the urge for freedom, relaxation taking root once more.

Just a few more moments, he thought.

She lifted her head, staring down at him. "I want you to see me, feel me, taste me." She ground forward with her hips, feeling him pulsate and ready to explode.

He arched his back, releasing another moan that echoed off the walls. No longer could he wait. This had to happen, now.

Just as he was about to give in to his gluttonous desires, the red blindfold ripped away from his sight. His hazy vision flowed through the room, adjusting to the dim lighting. Sabine sat upon his lap, eyes burning, but not with ecstasy. Fury scorched within her violet eyes. Four girls from downstairs also surrounded the bed, all leering down at him.

What the hell is this? Where is Adeline, the girl I bought?

While staring at the two girls on his right, a stinging pain sprouted in his abdomen. His sight shifted, trailing to his stomach. There, plunged deep into his flesh, was a dagger. Sabine's fingers shook as she squeezed the grip. This was no game. This was vengeance.

"For Eira." The words leaked through her locked jaw.

He recoiled from her, hearing the name and feeling the sharp pain spread throughout his core. As he did, the others raised their daggers and mirrored the same phrase. "For Eira."

They brought the daggers down in unison, piercing his chest, his abdomen. A river of life leaked from the wounds as they withdrew the blades, saturating the plush bed in a pond of crimson.

A scream bellowed from his lungs, blanketing the room in despair. With a pained expression, his eyes fluttered as he let out a groan, successfully tearing his arms away from the feeble knots. He cradled his stomach, his ribs. The agony burned inside, a smouldering wildfire raging through a valley.

He could feel his life slipping away, a candle's flame snuffed out. Slowly, he forced his welled eyes open. Madam Hollier stood to his left; his satchel drooped in her palm. She delivered a coy smile, watching him slip away, mocking him. "The pleasure is mine, Elric. Thank you for you patronage, old friend."

He rolled onto his back, grimacing with shock, suppressing the dark seeping in. Another scream leapt from his throat before he searched the room. His assailant, Sabine, had vacated the scene along with the others, but he could see two figures approaching, both clutching daggers. He knew the girl with the scars covering her cheek and forehead. And he also knew the young girl with the mousy hair and freckles.